AMISH GIRL'S CHRISTMAS

BOOK 1 AMISH FOSTER GIRLS

SAMANTHA PRICE

CHAPTER ONE

*Who knoweth not in all these that
the hand of the LORD hath wrought this?*
Job 12:9

*E*lizabeth ran from the house to the barn with two cookies clutched in her hand while snowflakes softly fell around her. Once she got safely into the barn without anyone calling her back, she looked at the house hoping no one would notice her missing—at least until she ate her snack. Spotting a bale of hay, she pulled it closer to the door. That way, she would see if anyone approached.

The white Amish farmhouse looked pretty as the snow settled on the roof. The Grabers' home wasn't large compared with some of their neighbors, but there were four small bedrooms, enough for the Grabers and their three foster children, of whom Elizabeth was one. She'd been with Gretchen and William Graber for ten years. Before that, she'd been placed with the Wallaces briefly and then the O'Briens. She much preferred Gretchen and William Graber as foster parents. If only there weren't so many chores all the time.

She stared at the smoke spiraling from the single chimney and breathed in deeply. The smoke mixed with the aroma of the baking bread, and the sight of the fresh snow gave Elizabeth a sense of comfort. Most of the memories of her parents were now faded, but she remembered some of their Christmases together.

Recollections of her father teaching her to skate on the ice were the clearest of them all.

He'd bundle her up and allow her to sit in the front seat of his truck while he drove to the skating rink. Then it seemed like they stayed on the ice for hours while he patiently taught her the proper movements— how to slide one leg out and then the other.

When she'd gotten it right and skated alone, she remembered her squeals of delight as her father cheered her on, grinning from ear-to-ear at her efforts.

Sadly, they only had a few seasons together.

Remembering those years tugged at her heart. Many years had passed since her parents had died in the accident. Fortunately, she had no memory of the accident and had been told she'd been thrown clear of the car during the wreck. Her parents weren't that lucky and had both died at the scene. Having no known relatives, Elizabeth was immediately placed into foster care.

She nibbled on the cookie while her eyes settled again on the smoke that came from the wood-burning stove in the kitchen. Elizabeth was continually amazed that one stove was able to generate enough warmth to heat the entire household.

When she'd finished the cookies, she dusted off the crumbs from her hands, pulled the hay back to where it had been, and then headed back to the Graber house where she lived with two other foster children, Megan and Tara, who were around the same age.

Gretchen's head whipped up from sharpening knives at the kitchen table when Elizabeth walked back inside.

"Don't you have work at the coffee shop this morning, Elizabeth?"

"No. I'm not scheduled for today."

Megan and Tara were sitting beside Gretchen, having a break from their chores.

"Where have you been?" Tara asked.

"I just stepped outside for a moment."

Megan, the quieter of the girls, asked, "Would you like some hot chocolate?"

"Yes, please." Elizabeth took a seat at the table, pleased she'd arrived back in time for another break from daily chores.

Megan was always doing things for others, and fussing over people like a mother hen. Tara was forever talking about boys, mostly when Gretchen was out of earshot.

Gretchen said, "I know it's hard for all of you at this time of year."

Elizabeth nodded. "I still miss my parents."

"At least you have some memories," Megan said as she poured the hot chocolate into a cup.

Elizabeth knew that Megan's father had died suddenly when she was a baby, and her widowed mother had been in poor health and unable to handle single-motherhood. There hadn't been any relatives who were able to help her mother or to give Megan a home.

"I know." Gretchen's eyes moistened in sympathy as she listened to the girls.

"Well, I've got no one to miss." Tara's words were firm and cold.

Tara had only been with them for three years, and had never known her parents. She'd been adopted twice and then twice given up when each family's circumstances had changed. Elizabeth had never asked and neither had she been told what Tara had gone through, but given her harsh exterior she guessed it was something horrid. The Grabers' house was a haven for the three of them. Unable to have children themselves, Gretchen and William opened their home to children who needed to be loved.

Megan looked out the window. "It's snowing, *Mamm!*"

Megan had adapted quickly to the Amish ways, calling her foster parents *Mamm* and *Dat*. Tara and Elizabeth called the Grabers *Onkel* William and *Ant* Gretchen. After all, they weren't Elizabeth's real mother and father, and Tara must've felt the same.

Something in Elizabeth's heart held her back from throwing herself into the Amish ways. Her parents weren't Amish, so she wasn't sure if this was where she belonged. Thinking about whether God had placed her with the Grabers because He wanted her to be Amish made her head spin sometimes. That would mean that He didn't prevent that dreadful accident, and He spared her so she'd be placed here, and thinking if all of that could be so...it then caused her to feel dreadfully guilty.

In a year or two, she'd have to make up her mind what to do. If she chose to live amongst the people in the world outside the community, where would she live? She had no known relatives, no connections to her parents. The only place now that felt like home was with the Grabers. Every Amish woman got married young—it was the Amish way to marry and have many children. The choice was clear—she'd have to find an Amish man to marry, or leave the Amish community and make her way as an outsider —an *Englischer*. She already had a job in a coffee shop, so that was a good start.

"Here you go, Elizabeth."

Elizabeth looked at the hot chocolate that Megan had just placed in front of her. *"Denke,* Megan."

"What are you girls doing today after your chores?" Gretchen asked.

"I'm going into town," Tara announced with a secret smile hinting around her lips.

Elizabeth guessed she was most likely going to meet a boy somewhere.

"What about you, Megan?"

"I think I'll just stay around here and catch up on my sewing."

Gretchen smiled at Megan's response. A real Amish girl would've most likely stayed home and sewed. Gretchen would prefer if the three of them stayed in the Amish community rather than go out into the world.

Elizabeth said to Gretchen, "I'm going ice-skating today. It's been a long time."

"Okay, *gut*. I know how you like your skating. I'm almost finished making the quilt I've been working on, so that's my project for today."

"Gut! We can sew together, *Mamm."*

Gretchen smiled warmly at Megan.

After a period of silence while they drank their hot drinks and ate cookies, Gretchen said, "Tara, you might as well take Elizabeth to wherever she's going to skate, and you can fetch her on your return. That way we only need use one buggy."

"Okay," Tara said. "I don't know exactly how long I'll be."

"Just come and get me whenever you're finished."

~

STARING OUT AT THE ICE, Elizabeth fought back tears. Two children playing in the snow near the pond provided a good distraction. Elizabeth knew she'd been like one of those carefree children many years ago.

"Okay, here I go," Elizabeth whispered looking down at the skates on her feet.

As soon as her foot hit the ice, joy rippled through her body. Elizabeth could never explain what it felt like to be on the ice. All she understood is that she'd never truly be happy if she didn't skate. It was like flying—as free as a bird.

She soon gathered speed at the edge of the frozen pond, listening to the steel hit the ice with each stride. Chips of ice flew behind her as she increased her speed and readied for what her father had called her 'special move.'

Lifting one leg into the air, Elizabeth stretched out her arms and leaned forward with her leg out behind her as far as it would go within the confines of her long dress. Allowing the momentum to move her, she floated on one skate with the bitter wind hitting her face, freezing her tears onto her cheeks. When she lowered her leg to slow down, applause rang out from behind her.

Startled, Elizabeth came to a halt as soon as she could and then spun around to see where the commotion was coming from. On the other side of the ice stood a young Amish man. Embarrassed, Elizabeth stood still, wiped her tears, and then moved off the ice.

"You're really good," he called out.

Elizabeth gave a nod in a polite response, before looking for her bag containing her boots. The man must've been a visitor to their community because she'd never seen him before. Out of the corner of her eye, she saw movement from his direction. A loud thud followed by a painful whimper echoed through the air. The man lay on the ice, holding his leg.

"Are you okay?" Elizabeth asked as she quickly moved toward him.

Reaching for Elizabeth's outstretched hand, he answered, "Bruised, but not broken. I hope."

Elizabeth helped him to his feet and led him off the ice.

"You sure you're okay?"

"Dumb move, I guess. I didn't think walking on the ice would be that hard."

"Well, why were you walking on it? Where are your skates?"

The man turned crimson and laughed. "I was walking to talk to you. I wasn't thinking straight."

Elizabeth's eyebrows flew up, "Talk to me? Why?" He was handsome and she guessed him to be twenty or a little older.

He sat on a wooden bench and looked up at her. "You looked sad. Are you okay?"

"I'm fine, and I have to go." She saw her bag, walked over to it and proceeded to take off her skates and put on her boots. She'd never been good about talking with strangers.

"Don't go yet."

"I should. I have people waiting for me."

"Well, wait," he said rubbing his leg, "I don't even know your name." He limped over to her.

Elizabeth paused, and he continued, "I'm Joseph." He held out his hand for her to shake.

Elizabeth gave his hand a quick shake while sadness surged through her. Joseph was her father's name and here she was at the ice, their special place. She willed herself not to cry.

"I'm Elizabeth. I should go." Turning to leave, a shiver ran through her body. She hoped it wasn't noticeable and started to walk away hoping that Tara would see she was already gone when she came to fetch her, and would go home too.

"Are you freezing?" Joseph asked.

"It's been so cold for so long, I've gotten used to it. Goodbye," she called over her shoulder as she walked faster.

"You shivered. So, if it's not the cold, then what is it?" Joseph moved to follow Elizabeth. Catching up to her, he continued, "Look, I'm not trying to be rude or anything. I just saw a girl I'd like to get to know and made a fool of myself before I could give her my name. Can we start over?"

Elizabeth stopped in her tracks and turned around. "Start what over? You fell. I helped you. I'm Elizabeth. You're..." Tears welled in her eyes and she swallowed hard.

"Oh! I'm sorry. Did I say something to upset you?" Joseph asked.

Embarrassed, Elizabeth wiped her tears. "*Nee*. Sorry. It's not you. It's...well; it's complicated. I...um...it's... Never mind." She picked up her pace, ashamed of herself for reacting the way that she had. It wasn't his fault that he had the same name as her father. If she were going to function normally, she'd have to learn to control her emotions. Aunt Gretchen was always telling her she let emotions get the better of her.

"You can't walk anywhere in this cold. I'll drive you wherever you're going. My buggy is behind those trees."

He was right; it was too cold to walk and if Gretchen knew she'd walked so far in the snow, she'd get into trouble. Squinting in the direction he was pointing, she made out the shape of a buggy behind the trees. Before she could refuse or accept his offer, she heard a buggy and was pleased to see that it was Tara coming to collect her.

"I have to go. That's my friend who's come to get me." She'd never been so pleased to see Tara.

"I hope we meet again, Elizabeth."

She didn't answer and moved faster to meet the buggy.

CHAPTER TWO

Yea, though I walk through the valley of the shadow of death, I will fear no evil: for thou art with me; thy rod and thy staff they comfort me.

Psalm 23:4

Eighteen years ago in an Englisch home.

"*Y*ou know, Janice, some women can only have girls."

Janice stared at her mother-in-law, trying to get over her dislike of the woman, but how could she do that when everything that proceeded out of the woman's cruel, thin mouth was designed to put her down?

"I'm sure it'll be a boy." Janice placed her hand on her large baby bump. She was only weeks away from giving birth; she already had two girls, and she knew her husband desperately wanted a boy.

"I hope so for your sake. Lyle has always wanted a boy to carry on the family name and take over the dynasty. I don't think I need to remind you, but when Lyle has a boy, he'll be Lyle Doyle the Fourth."

"I know. You remind me every single day." It had been Lyle's idea to have his mother come to live with them when his father died.

Charlotte Doyle pulled a lace handkerchief out of her dress and dabbed at the corners of her eyes. "My Lyle would've liked to have seen our son have at least one son. Janice, a boy is what you need to give your husband. Who will take over from him?"

"Lyle and I have always said we're stopping at three. It's dangerous with my blood group and he said he doesn't want to put me at risk for a fourth." She'd made that up, the bit about the blood group, hoping it would put an end to Charlotte's rantings.

"You hear all the time of marriages that break down over these things."

Janice's heart pricked with fear. "What things?"

"Women who can't have boys. Their husbands divorce them and try again with another wife. There are many women who'd gladly marry him you know."

"Why would you say something like that to me?" Janice wasn't usually so outspoken, but she had grown weary of the woman's constant jibes.

Charlotte pursed her lips. "As I said, some women can only have girls."

"I believe that biologically speaking, it's something in the man's sperm that determines the sex of the child."

Charlotte gasped and now was using her lace handkerchief to fan herself. "How could you say those vulgar words out loud, Janice?"

"What, 'sex?' I'm not talking about the act; I'm talking about sex in the sense of boy or girl. And if you're talking about sperm, it's the sperm that determines the sex."

"There you go again." Charlotte averted her eyes as though she were terribly disappointed. "It's not necessary to say those words in polite company. I'll leave you to think about your actions while I have a lie down."

"Okay."

When Charlotte was halfway out of the room, she turned around. "I just don't want to see Lyle disappointed, if you have another girl. That'll be the third time he'll have been disappointed." Charlotte turned back and continued through the doorway.

Once she was gone, Janice was able to relax. Although Charlotte was annoying and probably deliberately trying to upset her, what if she was right about her husband leaving her for another woman?

Three of Janice's friends had been divorced after their husbands left them for younger women. At every social event she and Lyle had been to, women threw themselves at him even with her standing right next to him. What would these women be like if she hadn't been there? It was a constant worry, particularly with Lyle going on so many business trips so far from home.

To make matters worse, Lyle had often talked about having a son who would be able to take over his business concerns. How she hoped their baby would be a boy.

IT WAS early Christmas morning when Janice's water broke. Her husband hadn't been able to get home the day before because the airports were closed with the snow. He was held up in New York. This was one birth she'd have to go through alone.

She called her sister, Jane, to look after her two girls, and as soon as she arrived, Janice took a taxi to the birthing center where her good friend and homebirth midwife, Margaret, would deliver her third child.

When she arrived, she got herself settled into one of the rooms and called her husband.

"I'm still trying to get there. I've hired a car."

"How did you get a car? Aren't the roads closed too?"

"Don't worry about me. Concentrate on you and the baby."

"Lyle, don't be reckless. Don't drive too quickly."

He chuckled. "I'll be safe. Here's hoping for a boy."

"What if she's a girl?"

"It'll be a boy! I've got to go now; they're bringing the car around."

The call ended and Janice placed the cell phone down. She noticed he didn't answer when she asked if he minded having another girl. His mother was right; he desperately wanted a son.

JANICE LAY there with her baby daughter in her arms. She kissed her gently on her forehead and breathed in the scent of the newborn. As soon as Margaret had delivered Janice's baby, she'd headed to the other room to deliver another baby. Janice felt sympathy as she listened to the other woman groan and scream.

Tears ran down her cheeks. The birth should've been a celebration, but disappointment was all she felt. It wasn't right and she knew it. Her baby was beautiful and she was healthy, but as she was so hoping for a boy, she didn't feel the connection to this baby that she'd felt with her other two girls. It should've been a time for celebration, but it wasn't.

Soon the midwife came back into the room. "That's two births in one day."

"Two on Christmas day? I never really thought that I'd have her on Christmas day."

Margaret walked over to her. "I'll put her in the crib and help you to the bathroom. Then she can have her first feeding."

"Okay, but I'll be all right to walk by myself."

"Are you sure?"

"Yes. I'm feeling okay." Janice walked down the hall to the bathroom. When she came back, she heard the other baby crying and peeped into the room. The other woman looked up and saw her. She was alone too.

"Hello," she said smiling warmly.

"Hi." Janice moved closer and looked at the baby in her arms. "What did you have?"

The woman looked down at her baby. "He's a boy."

"Can I see him?"

"Yes. Come in."

Janice sat down on the chair next to the bed, staring at the beautiful baby boy. If only she'd had a boy. "I had a girl. My husband desperately wanted a boy." She wondered whether her husband would be able to hide his disappointment.

The woman studied her for a moment. "Are you Janice Doyle?"

"Yes, I am." It was no surprise that the woman knew who she was. She and her husband were well known in the area.

"I recognize you from the magazines."

Janice burst out crying, covering her face with her hands.

"I'm sorry. Did I say something wrong?"

"No." She wiped her eyes. "It's just that my husband desperately wanted a boy. He's driving back here now and I have to tell him we had another girl and I don't want to go through it all again trying for a boy."

The woman looked at her sympathetically.

Janice sniffed, looked up at the ceiling and blinked rapidly. "I'm sorry. I don't know why I'm telling you all this."

"How badly do you want a boy?"

"Very badly, but it's too late now."

"Maybe not!"

Janice sniffed again. "What do you mean?"

"Would you consider swapping? I mean I might be enticed to do so."

"I couldn't. No. Not at all."

"Think about it. My husband's truck is stuck in the snow somewhere and he doesn't know if we had a boy or a girl."

Janice could scarcely believe what she was hearing, but it might work. "Well, the only person who knows is Margaret and she'll keep quiet if I ask her." Janice shook her head. "I can't believe I'm considering this."

"I won't do it for nothing at all. I know how rich you people are and if you want it to happen you can pay."

"Would you tell your husband?"

"As long as we have a child, it doesn't make a difference where she came from. And then there would be the money. We've never had anything. We've always had one struggle after another. If you take him, I know he'll have everything he ever wanted. We can't give him anything. We could never pay for college."

This was a solution. If this worked, everyone would win. Her heart pumped hard within her chest. "How much money? I could pay you a lump sum and then send you money every month. Enough money for your whole family to live on."

"Won't your husband notice that much money gone?"

"I have my own money. I don't need to use my husband's."

"Let me see your baby and make sure she's healthy."

Janice put her hand on her chest. "Should we do this?"

"Let me see your baby and I'll tell you."

Janice walked back into the room.

Margaret was with her baby and she looked over at Janice. "Where were you?"

"Talking to the woman in the next room. What do you know about her?"

"They don't have much money. I'm not charging them. She's got a fear of hospitals, and a doctor friend of mine asked me if I'd look after her. They're some distant degree of relative to him."

"Are they good people?"

"Yes. I believe so."

"How poor are they?"

"Very." Margaret looked at the baby. "Are you ready to feed her now?"

"I'm just going to take her to show the woman next door. I was just looking at her baby and she wants to see mine."

Margaret eyed her suspiciously. "Have you called Lyle yet? He'll be anxious to know how you are and to hear that the baby arrived safely."

"No. And if he calls here, tell him I haven't had it yet."

Margaret recoiled. "Why?"

"You've got to trust me." Janice took her baby into her arms and walked her to the lady in the next room. "Here she is," Janice said showing the woman her baby.

"Can I hold her?"

Janice put the baby girl into her arms and looked at the boy now in the crib, wondering if she'd be able to love him as her own.

"Pick him up," the woman insisted.

Janice picked up the little boy and held him close. Yes, the plan could work.

"We'd still each have a baby to love."

"Would you look after her as though she was your own?" Janice asked.

"I would. And I'd know you could give him everything that Joseph and I never could give him."

"You'll love her, though, won't you?"

"I wanted a girl." The woman chuckled. "I'll love her and keep her safe. Now, how much money are we talking?"

Janice, holding the other woman's baby, negotiated a large settlement and then ongoing monthly payments. The woman had to agree that she'd never tell anyone of the swap.

"I need money today or there's no deal. How will I know you won't change your mind?"

"I'll call and get one of my staff to bring money in from home. Can I carry him back to my room to use my cell phone?"

"Go ahead. I'll keep her here."

When she walked back into the room, Margaret looked at her. "Are you ready to feed her yet?" She jumped to her feet. "What are you doing, Janice? That's not your baby!"

"I need to tell you something. Sit down."

She sat Margaret down and explained her intentions.

"No, Janice! You can't be serious."

"I am and I'm going to do it."

"Why? Does it matter if you have a girl or a boy? You'll be found out!"

"No, I won't. If I'm found out, the payments to Lillian and her husband stop. I certainly won't tell anyone and neither will you."

"I can't believe you're serious. It's illegal. I'll lose my credibility. No one will use my services again and I've spent a fortune on this place." Margaret glared at her. "You'll regret this."

"I won't. I'll raise him as my own. No one will find out. You can't tell anyone."

"I can't let you do it, Janice. It's madness! You'll be found out!"

"Don't forget who loaned you the money for this place."

Margaret's eyes grew wide.

"What would happen if I called in the loan?"

"You wouldn't."

"I'm desperate. You've got to look the other way. Please?"

Deep lines appeared in Margaret's forehead as she placed both hands on her cheeks.

Janice put her hand lightly on her friend's arm. "Stay there and we'll talk more. I've just got to make a phone call."

Janice called home and had her housekeeper stop cooking the Christmas dinner and bring money in from the safe. Her housekeeper wouldn't ask what the money was for and she couldn't even let her sister, Jane, in on such a secret. Jane would pull the 'big sister card' and refuse to allow her to go through with it. She might even tell Lyle of her intentions. No—the fewer people who knew about this, the better.

When Janice had hung up from giving Magda her instructions, Margaret said, "You're serious? I can't believe it."

"Margaret, are you going to keep quiet about this? I need to know now because this is going ahead. Otherwise…"

"It seems I don't have a choice. I just hope this doesn't blow up in all our faces."

CHAPTER THREE

Once the deal was done and Margaret had been sworn to secrecy, Janice picked up her cell phone and called her husband. "Lyle, we have a boy!"

"I was so worried when I didn't hear from you. Is everything okay?"

"Everything went perfectly. The birth was a bit longer than the other two, but he's a boy, so he took a little more time." Janice bit her lip hoping her husband wouldn't detect the lie from over the phone. He was normally pretty good at reading her. "How far away are you?"

"Another hour, I'd say. I've been held up along the roads. I just called home and Jane said the girls are fine. She also said you called Magda to the birthing center. Are you sure everything's all right?"

"Yes. I just needed some things from home that I forgot."

"I'll see you soon."

"I can barely hear you."

"Don't be concerned if you call and can't reach me for the next several minutes. I can already hear crackling in the phone."

"Okay. Are you pleased that we finally had a boy?"

"I'm over the moon! I always wanted a boy and now we finally have one."

His last words faded away and then the phone went dead. Janice smiled, pleased that she had made her husband happy. As far as she was concerned, this was a win-win situation for all of them. Her daughter would be raised in a home with plenty of money and a lot of love, and the baby boy would be raised with the same.

She went back into the other woman's room with the baby boy, so each could say a final goodbye to her child.

When Lyle brought Janice home the next morning after they had both stayed the night at the birthing center, Janice wanted nothing more than to see the look on her mother-in-law's face.

Lyle was delighted with his son and the Simpsons were happy with their daughter.

Lyle pushed the front door open and Janice walked into the sitting room where Charlotte was waiting.

"Well, let me see him," the old woman said in her usual demanding way.

Janice sat down next to her, so her mother-in-law could get a good look at him.

"He's much bigger than the girls were."

"That's because he's a boy."

"He doesn't have the Doyle ears."

Lyle laughed at his mother's comment. "He has his own ears, Mother, and they *are* Doyle ears." Lyle sat opposite them.

"When you were born, you looked like all your father's baby photos. I just don't see a resemblance."

Lyle laughed again, amused at his mother. "He'll grow up looking like the rest of us. Don't you worry."

Charlotte gave Janice a sidelong glance.

"I told you we'd have a boy, Charlotte."

Janice's sister, Jane, walked in just then with the two girls who were eager to see their new baby brother.

Eight years later.

JANICE'S DEAL with the Simpsons had gone according to plan for eight years, until the day Janice got a call from her bank.

"What do you mean the money's stopped going in? How can that happen? I made arrangements for the money to go in every week."

"I know, but the account has been closed."

Janice's heart froze. "When did that happen?"

"A few weeks ago."

"Why? Do you know why it closed? And why am I only finding out about this now?"

"I'm sorry, Mrs. Doyle. Sometimes money doesn't go through due to some glitch, but I checked when it bounced back and found that the account's been closed. I've got no way of knowing why it was closed because the Simpsons named on the account are with a different bank."

"I see."

"Perhaps you can make contact with the owner of the account and they can give you an alternate account?"

"That's what I'll have to do. Thank you." Janice ended the call. The only thing had to be that the Simpsons were after more money. Pain gnawed at her stomach. She had an address for them. Since they hadn't made contact yet, she'd have to knock on their door, talk to them face-to-face and see how much they wanted. Mr. Simpson had learned of the swap at the birthing center, and had been fine with it after his wife had talked him around.

The next morning, when the three children were in school, Janice drove to the address she had for the Simpsons. When she stopped in front of the house, there was a for sale sign out front. She got out of the car and knocked on the door. When no one answered after several more knocks, Janice walked around the side of the house and stopped to peep in the windows. There was no furniture—the place was abandoned.

When she got back to the car, she picked up her cell and called the number on the sign. The agent refused to give any details about where the people had moved.

The next stop was the Simpsons' bank. She went to their branch and inquired as to whether they'd opened another account. Again, she was met with a dead end. The bank refused to give her details due to privacy reasons.

Janice drove home defeated. Then it occurred to her that if the Simpsons needed more money, they'd have to contact her soon.

After weeks had gone by with no word from the Simpsons, she wrote a letter to their old address hoping the letter might be forwarded to their new one.

Four weeks later, the letter was returned.

CHAPTER FOUR

The thief comes only to steal and kill and destroy;
I have come that they may have life,
and have it to the full.
John 10:10

The present day.

he day turned to night and Elizabeth still hadn't shaken the overwhelming feeling of sorrow. Lying in her warm bed, she stared out the window and watched the snowflakes softly falling. It wasn't long before her thoughts turned to her parents. Deep down, she knew that they would not want her to wallow in grief to the point she could not enjoy the simple pleasures of life. She knew from being raised

Amish for so many years that death was a part of life, but that didn't stop her from missing her parents. *God, please help me to be stronger, and help to ease the pain I feel inside.*

Her mind turned to the man she'd met earlier in the day. Elizabeth normally wouldn't have minded if someone had seen her cry, but something about crying in front of him made her uncomfortable. Closing her eyes, she pictured the young man before her, and soon when sleep overtook her, he moved into her dreams.

THE SUN SHONE brightly through the bedroom window as Elizabeth popped out of bed to get ready for work. Shaking the cobwebs out of her head, she rushed around her room unaware that she was humming.

Gretchen knocked on her bedroom door and entered carrying ice skates. "You left these in the way downstairs."

"I'm sorry."

"Don't put down, put away. Just remember that."

"I will."

Gretchen folded her arms and leaned against the door frame. "Are you going skating today?"

"No. Yesterday didn't go so well. I have work, and then Megan is meeting me before we go to the singing at the Yoders.'"

"Take the buggy today. *Onkel* William is hitching it up for you now."

"Are you sure?"

"*Jah*. I'll have him take Megan to the coffee shop this afternoon and then the two of you can go from there."

"*Denke.*"

Gretchen nodded. "Have a good day, then. Be careful out there on the roads; go slow. And wear your coat; you don't want to catch a cold."

Elizabeth took the skates, deciding that she could throw them into the back of the buggy just in case they could skate somewhere tonight.

AFTER HER WORK THAT DAY, Elizabeth looked around the busy coffee shop and found a seat at the end of a large communal table and waited for Megan.

Being early and knowing that Megan was always late, Elizabeth ordered a cappuccino and waited. Her thoughts were a million miles away when someone sat across from her. She looked over to see that the person was not Megan; it was the man from the day before.

"Hi," he said.

She smiled "Hi."

"What were you deep in thought about?" Joseph asked.

"Hey, look, I'm really so..."

He raised his hand signaling her to stop. Smiling, he held out his hand, "My name's Joseph. What's yours?"

"Elizabeth."

"I don't know how many beginnings we have to have, but at least you didn't shiver that time. I must not be as scary as I was yesterday." Joseph removed his hat and ran his large hand through his hair.

"You're not scary. I didn't think that."

"*Jah*, you did. That's why you shivered. It's okay, you know. I'm not begging for you to help me up today."

"Elizabeth."

Elizabeth looked up to see Megan.

"There you are. Late as usual."

"I can't stay to go with you today. I'm sorry, I have to help *Mamm* with something."

Before Elizabeth could say anything or introduce Joseph, Megan was out the door and disappearing up the road. Megan wasn't comfortable around men; neither was Elizabeth, but Megan was painfully shy.

"I can stay and keep you company," Joseph said.

She had to laugh at him. It seemed he wasn't going to let up. They spent the next hour talking and laughing. Joseph filled her in on all the details of how his family had just come to Lancaster County. Elizabeth felt more relaxed with him now that she knew he was a new member of her community.

The crowd around them came and went and neither noticed until Tara sat down in the seat next to her.

"I'm Tara," she said, her beady eyes fixed on Joseph.

Joseph shook her hand, his eyes scarcely leaving Elizabeth's. "Nice to meet you."

"So, I haven't seen you before. Are you one of the new *familye* who just moved into the community?" Tara inquired while staring intently at him.

"*Jah*, we've just moved here. I guess I'll meet everyone this Sunday at the gathering."

Tara raised her eyebrows. "Oh? Why did your *familye* move here and where have you come from?"

Elizabeth rolled her eyes. Up to this point, all that she had learned about Joseph was that he couldn't ice-skate, he was learning the building trade from his uncle, Kevin, and he'd just moved here.

"Excuse my friend, she's a little nosy," Elizabeth said in a teasing tone.

"Curious and inquisitive. Interested, but not nosy."

Tara didn't move despite the look Elizabeth gave her for asking so many questions.

"Well?" Tara said, turning back to face Joseph.

Joseph obliged and filled the girls in on the details surrounding his family. And more about himself.

"So, you're going to be a builder? Will you make a lot of money?" Tara asked.

Elizabeth nudged Tara, frowning at her. Tara and Megan were total opposites. Megan could barely speak to the man and had run out, whereas Tara was so bold she was asking far too many questions.

Joseph didn't have time to say more before a crowd swarmed in singing Christmas songs.

"Oh yeah, that reminds me," Tara said at the end of the first carol. "They're having a singing tonight at the Yoders' *haus* and they're starting early tonight. You going?" Talking a mile a minute, Tara continued,

"Oh, Joseph, you will love this. The Yoders have a big Christmas tree on their property, and they have a big celebration with cider and hot chocolate. You have to go; every young person in the community will be there."

Looking at Elizabeth, Joseph asked, "Shall we go see?"

Shrugging, Elizabeth wondered if she should go home now that Megan had gone home. "I'm not ready for Christmas yet."

"You told Aunt Gretchen you were going." Tara ignored her excuse and grabbed Elizabeth by the arm, tugging her out of her seat, begging, "Let's go! We can't miss this. It's a tradition."

"Okay, okay. *Onkel* William loaned me the buggy today. I can take us all in that."

"Are you girls cousins?" He looked between the two of them.

"It's a long story," Tara said. "What do you say, Joseph?"

"I brought my buggy," he responded. "It's just outside."

Never short on ideas of how to organize people, Tara made a suggestion. "Elizabeth and I will follow you to your *haus*, then you leave your buggy there and come with us. At the end of the night, we'll take you home."

As they followed Joseph back to his house, Elizabeth had to listen to Tara tell her what a nice man Joseph was.

"And he likes you, Elizabeth. That cool and calm exterior is reeling him in just like a fish with a hook through it."

Elizabeth pulled a face, not liking the images that sprung to her mind. "I don't know about that. I barely know him. He seems okay."

"More than okay if you ask me. Now we'll be the first ones in the community to see where he lives."

Elizabeth giggled at her friend. Life was never boring when Tara was around.

"Wasn't Megan coming?"

"She met me at the coffee shop and then ran away when she saw Joseph."

Tara shook her head. "We really must do something with her, or she'll be living with Gretchen and William forever and a day."

"She'll be okay."

"I hope so."

CHAPTER FIVE

Trust in the Lord with all your heart
and lean not on your own understanding.
Proverbs 3:5

*I*t was mostly the young people who had gathered at the Yoders' house.

The three of them joined the crowd in singing the lively hymns. Joseph bellowed out as many words of the songs as he could remember. Within a few seconds, Elizabeth did her best to shrug off her sadness and put the loss of her parents to one side.

When there was a break in the singing, Tara finally left them alone.

Joseph turned to Elizabeth. "Tell me about yourself."

"You already know everything. There's not much more to tell."

"Somehow, I don't believe that. Let's go for a walk away from all this noise."

As they walked, Elizabeth felt comfortable enough to tell him about how she came to be in the Amish community. "I wasn't born in the community. The Grabers took me in ten years ago. I was eight when my parents died."

"That's awful. I'm sorry."

Elizabeth nodded and kept talking. "Neither of my parents had any relatives, which I find really strange. Anyway, that's how I ended up in foster care. I was briefly at a couple of places before I came to the Grabers' home. I don't remember the other places much—just vague recollections."

"What did you mean about finding it strange that your family had no relatives?"

"I didn't think about it as a child, but often when parents die, their child would be taken in by a relation. Neither of them had one. Now that I'm in the community, it's hard to think that a married couple wouldn't have had at least one relation between the two of them."

"Have you looked into it? They could both have been orphans or something."

She shook her head. "I haven't, but I think I will. I barely remember what they looked like. My memories of them are so fuzzy. I remember how they made me feel and that's the clearest thing—the feelings."

"How did they make you feel?"

Elizabeth glanced up into Joseph's face. No one else had ever cared to ask her so many questions. "I guess I felt safe and I felt loved. They were my protectors, and my teachers. I remember my father teaching me how to tie my shoelaces and my mother telling me how to spell words."

"Maybe if you look them up and do some research you could find some relatives somewhere."

"Do you think so?"

"I do."

"I don't think the Grabers would like me doing that. They want me to stay in the community forever."

"What do you want to do?"

She shook her head. "I think I would feel better finding out more about my parents. All I know is that my father drove trucks and my mother stayed home." When Elizabeth heard Tara's loud laughter, she looked back and saw that they'd gone far. "We should start back." She turned around.

Joseph turned as well and together they walked back to the house.

"It looks so beautiful from here," Joseph said.

Elizabeth looked ahead to see the Yoders' yard lit up. Christmas candles hung in the trees and luminous colored lanterns were strung everywhere. The snow sparkled and the whole place glistened like a wonderland.

"It's so pretty at night."

Tara walked up to join them when they got back to the yard.

"Would you like a cup of cider?" Joseph asked Elizabeth, but both girls answered, "Yes," at the same time. With a hint of a smile on his face, he walked off.

Tara nudged Elizabeth, and asked, "What's wrong with you?"

Elizabeth had known Tara long enough to know what she was getting at. "I've only just met him."

"Have some fun for once! He's most likely a gift from *Gott;* he's following you around, and you're frowning. That's not the Elizabeth I used to know. Make her reappear before you ruin your chances with that man." Tara stopped talking as Joseph returned with the cider.

Suspicious of Elizabeth's blushing, he asked, "Were you talking about me?"

"*Nee.*" Elizabeth knew she answered too quickly.

Tara leaned in toward Joseph. "Hey, Joseph, you know, Elizabeth loves to ice-skate. Do you skate? I heard they were decorating around the pond, too, tonight. Maybe you two should walk over and have a look."

Rolling her eyes, Elizabeth quipped, "She's so subtle, isn't she?"

Joseph turned to face Elizabeth, his blue eyes shimmering under the lights, "That's actually a pretty good idea. Do you girls want to go see?"

Tara excused herself and Elizabeth was left alone again with Joseph.

"Sorry about that. She's very forthright. Tara lives with me and so does the girl at the coffee shop earlier today. We're all the foster children of the Grabers," Elizabeth said.

Joseph nodded.

"Did I mention I worked at the coffee shop? Did you come there today to see me?"

He laughed. *"Nee,* I had no idea. I just wanted *kaffe.* Is that where you work?"

"Jah. I'd finished working and was waiting for Megan. Now I feel like a fool. I'm an idiot to think you were trying to find me."

"I was hoping we could spend some more time together. It was a nice surprise to see you there. I thought I'd have to wait until one of the Sunday meetings."

Elizabeth blushed.

They walked toward the pond on the edge of the Yoders' property.

"You seem down, Elizabeth. I know it's wretched about your parents; is that why?"

"It's just this time of year that makes me sad. I'm sorry, I didn't know it showed so much."

"It does."

"Christmas Day is my birthday. More than any other time of the year, I think about my parents at this time."

"That's understandable."

Elizabeth told Joseph what she remembered about her parents. Wisps of wavy hair sprang out from underneath her prayer *kapp* every time the wind picked up.

Joseph gently pushed the strands of hair away from her face.

Elizabeth stopped speaking long enough to take in the gentleness of his touch.

"*Denke*," she said.

"For what?" Joseph asked.

"For listening. That was sweet of you."

The iced-over pond was only a couple of yards away from them. They stood still and watched the many rays of light from the lanterns dance on the ice.

"It's beautiful, isn't it?" Joseph asked.

A lone tear fell from Elizabeth's eye. "It's beautiful." As if on cue, small flakes of snow fell around them.

Elizabeth and Joseph couldn't help but giggle with delight as they stared up into the dark sky.

"This might be the craziest thing I've ever done, but do you have your skates with you?"

Elizabeth replied, "They're in my buggy. Why?"

"Can you teach me to skate?" Joseph asked.

Elizabeth laughed in surprise and then, looking at his large feet, she said, "My skates won't fit on your feet."

Joseph laughed. "I know that. Let's go back and have a word with the Yoders. They've got about nine children, some of them as big as me. I'll see if they've got some skates I can borrow."

"Okay, let's do it.

Just as Joseph had said, the Yoder boys all had skates and they were only too happy for him to borrow a pair.

Once Elizabeth had her skates under her arm, she tried to keep up with Joseph as he strode with determination back toward the pond.

"You really want to do this?" she asked him.

"*Jah*, I can't wait to glide across the ice," Joseph said.

"It's not that easy, you know. It takes a while before you stop falling over."

"Depends."

Laughter escaped Elizabeth's lips. "What do you mean? Depends on what?"

"Whether you're a *gut* teacher or not."

"That's not fair. If you're a bad skater are you going to blame me?"

Joseph leaned down at the edge of the pond and strapped on the skates. "If you're a good teacher, I won't be a bad skater."

OVER THE NEXT SEVERAL DAYS, Elizabeth and Joseph met every day. Sometimes they met after she finished work and other times they met at the ice to skate.

Elizabeth, standing at the edge of the ice, watched now as Joseph glided across the surface of the pond. He'd had a few falls and he still looked wobbly, but the fact that he had learned to skate relatively well in just a few short weeks either proved that he was a natural or that Elizabeth's father had taught her well.

Stopping near her, Joseph asked, "Well, we've officially been dating for almost two weeks now. So, with Christmas only a week away, what would you like for a Christmas present?"

"Dating? Is that what we've been doing?"

"*Jah.*"

"Oh."

"What's the matter?" he asked.

"I thought there should've been some official time that we had a conversation about it. Were we dating, or are we just friends?"

He smiled at her. "Friends and more than friends. At least that's what I'm hoping."

She gave a little giggle and skated into the middle of the pond hearing the sounds of him close behind her. Stopping suddenly, she waited to see if he'd be able to stop just as fast. He did, and then she spun around to face him.

"Answer my question?" he said.

"About a gift?"

He nodded.

"I have everything I want." She stared into his eyes wondering if he might kiss her.

"And I'm pretty happy too. You came into my life, and you've taught me to skate. What more could a man want?"

Elizabeth could feel her cheeks burning as her heart pounded in anticipation. What she wanted for Christmas was simply to feel his lips upon hers, but she wasn't about to say so.

"You're no longer that sad girl I first saw, alone on the ice."

"I'm not sad."

"I so wanted to impress you that first time that I saw you, and I fell flat on my face."

Elizabeth laughed. "*Jah*, I was sad that day. Sometimes I get like that."

"Are you happy with the Grabers?"

"I am. I love them and I'm really close with Tara and Megan. We're a family."

"I know. I've seen that. Now, shall we skate?"

"Aren't you tired of skating yet?"

"Not when I can skate with you." He skated away. "First one to the edge of the ice is a winner."

He always said that and she always managed to overtake him.

CHAPTER SIX

"For I know the plans I have for you," declares the Lord,
"plans to prosper you and not to harm you,
plans to give you hope and a future."
Jeremiah 29:11

"*S*leepy head!"

Elizabeth woke up to a pillow being thrown on her head. She pushed it away and opened one eye to see Tara. "What are you doing?"

"Waking you up. Aren't you working today?"

"Yep." Elizabeth rolled over trying to grab another couple minutes of sleep.

"It's time to get up. You've got to take me to work today."

Tara had just gotten a job at one of the Amish quilt stores, not far from the coffee shop.

"What time is it?"

"A few minutes past seven."

"Okay. Just give me a few more minutes."

Then the blankets were ripped off her.

"Leave me alone!"

"Wake up now!"

Elizabeth sat up. There was no use arguing with Tara. "Okay. I'm up. Make me some *kaffe?*"

"Okay, as long as you don't go back to bed when I'm gone."

"I won't."

When Tara walked out of the room, Elizabeth rubbed her eyes. She'd been unable to sleep very much, her mind busy thinking about Joseph and the future they might share together. They'd get married soon so they could have children when they were still young, and they'd buy a little house and build on to it as their family grew. The idea of making a choice between the

Amish community and the *Englisch* world was a dim memory. Joseph was her future, she was certain of it.

As she slowly changed out of her nightdress and into her dress and apron, she daydreamed some more about Joseph. Would he come into the coffee shop for a quick bite to eat as he did some days? She hoped he would.

She pulled on black stockings before she dragged a brush through her long hair, wishing she'd braided it the night before. It was always snarly if it wasn't braided overnight. When the tangles cleared and the brush finally went right through smoothly, she tossed her brush down on the chest of drawers. After she'd divided her hair evenly in two, she braided one side and then the other before winding the braids and pinning them against her head. Lastly, she placed her prayer *kapp* on her head.

"There you are," Gretchen said as Elizabeth entered the kitchen. "Tara tells me you're taking her to work?"

"*Jah.* That's our plan."

"And she's bringing me home too," Tara said.

"Okay. I can do that I guess, but I finish at three."

"I finish at four, so you'll have to wait."

Elizabeth yawned. "Okay. Where's that *kaffe?*"

Tara put a mug in front of her while Gretchen placed a plate of pancakes on the table for everyone to help themselves. William had already gone to work early that morning. As soon as Megan walked in and sat down, everyone dove for the pancakes.

JUST AS THE lunch crowd had died down and Elizabeth was wiping down tables in the coffee shop, a well-dressed man walked in. He sat down and looked at a menu. Elizabeth finished clearing a table and took the stack of plates back to the kitchen to give him time to make his selection.

When she came out, Cathy, a girl she worked with, nodded toward the man. "You serve him, I bet he'll give you a good tip."

"Why don't you?"

"I don't do well with those rich types."

Elizabeth walked over to him. "Hello, have you had enough time to look at the menu?"

He looked up at her and then his jaw dropped open.

She stepped back, not knowing what to do. It frightened her the way he was ogling her.

"Do you know what you want to order, or shall I come back in a few minutes?"

"I'm sorry I'm staring. You look exactly like my youngest daughter. It's uncanny."

"Oh, a few people say I look familiar. I guess I've got one of those faces. Did you want to have something to eat?"

He placed the menu on the table without taking his eyes from her. "I'll have a flat white on skim."

"Nothing to eat?"

He rubbed his forehead. "Just give me something. I don't know what. I can't think straight. Get me whatever you think is good."

She nodded and hurried away. She gave an order into the kitchen for a beef pie with salad, and began to make his coffee.

"What did he say?" Cathy whispered.

"He was weird. You take his food to him. He makes me uncomfortable."

"He likes you. You'll get a good tip."

"I don't want a tip that way."

Cathy dug her in the ribs, nearly causing Elizabeth to spill the milk she was pouring into the coffee. Because the rush hour was over, Cathy and she were the only waitresses left working.

"Please, Cathy? I'll return the favor."

"Okay, we'll go halves in the tip if he leaves one, which he will. He's rich. I can tell."

"Okay, we'll go halves, but I don't want to talk to him again."

Cathy gave a little giggle as Elizabeth passed her his coffee.

She watched from behind the coffee machine as Cathy made her way back to the man.

"Where's the other girl?" she heard the man say.

Elizabeth crouched down behind the counter.

"Working in the back," Cathy replied.

"What's her name?"

"Elizabeth Simpson."

Elizabeth covered her mouth wishing Cathy hadn't given out her name.

Cathy hurried back to the kitchen when the meal order was called out, and then she took the food back to the man. While Cathy wiped down more of the vacant tables, Elizabeth stayed in the background wishing the man would leave.

When he finished eating, he called for the bill and Cathy left it with him. He stood up and pulled some notes from his pocket, put them on the table, and placed a cup over the corner. Then he left but not without having another look around for Elizabeth. He caught her eye and stared at her intently before he left.

Cathy wasted no time running over to his table to see how big his tip was. She grabbed the notes and hurried back to Elizabeth.

"He's left a two hundred dollar tip."

"That must be an accident. Go after him."

"Are you insane? He's a rich man. He meant to give this tip to us. Well, to you, but you agreed to halves. I think the man's in love with you."

"Yeah, well, did you have to give him my name?"

"There's no harm in that. Don't you see yourself with a rich sugar daddy?"

"No! I like Joseph."

"Boring! You're not really Amish. What's to stop you having a better life?"

Elizabeth raised her eyebrows at Cathy. Cathy was born and raised Amish and was getting married in January.

"Don't you think I should stay in the community?"

"I suppose so."

"I'm just glad that man's gone. I didn't like the way he was staring at me. He said I looked like his daughter. That means he knows he's old enough to be my father."

Cathy passed her one hundred dollars, kept one hundred for herself, and placed the remainder in the till for the meal. "Not bad. One hundred dollars because he liked the look of you."

"Creepy." Elizabeth shook her head while wondering what to do with the hundred dollars. It would certainly come in handy for buying Christmas gifts.

CHAPTER SEVEN

For in this hope we were saved.
Now hope that is seen is not hope. For who hopes for what he
sees? But if we hope for what we do not see, we wait for it with
patience.
Romans 8: 24-25

Across town.

anice ran to meet her husband when he walked into the house.

She threw her arms around his neck and kissed him. "You're early."

"Where are Felicity and Georgia?"

"Georgia's just come home and Felicity is still at work." Their son, Lyle IV, was in college away from home.

Seeing the distracted look on his face, she asked, "Is something wrong?"

He shook his head. "I've just had the weirdest thing happen. I need a drink."

"I'll pour us some whiskey and you can tell me about it."

When they were seated with drinks in their hands, Lyle said, "I saw a young woman today and she looked the spitting image of Georgia."

Janice took a gulp of her whiskey. "Where was she?"

"She was at a coffee shop. She's an Amish woman."

Janice laughed and was suddenly relieved. The Simpsons weren't Amish.

"You should come back and see her."

"No. I couldn't do that. Did you talk to her?"

He gave a laugh. "I think I scared the poor girl. I was staring at her and I told her how much she looked like one of my daughters. If I'd seen her from a distance, I'd have been dead sure it was Georgia."

"Was she wearing Amish clothes?"

"Yes, she had on the whole garb. I should've taken a photo."

"What were you doing there?"

"I'd just finished a meeting with a lawyer. I heard your voice in my head going mad at me for continually forgetting lunch and that's when I saw the place."

Janice took a sip of scotch.

He shook his head. "I still can't believe it."

"Believe what?" Charlotte walked into the room and sat down with them.

"Hello, Mother. I was just telling Janice that I saw a young woman who looked almost exactly like Georgia."

"How old was she?"

"I didn't ask." He laughed. "I think my reaction scared the poor woman half to death. She was Amish, and I guess they're private people."

Charlotte glanced at Janice and then looked back at her son. "If you had to guess how old would you say?"

"A little younger than Georgia."

"Where did you see her?"

"Charlotte, it doesn't really matter. It's all a fuss about nothing. There are many people who look like others.

They say everyone has a double somewhere in the world. Georgia's just happens to live close by," Janice said.

Georgia walked into the room. "Did I hear my name?"

Charlotte said, "Your father is just telling us that he met your double." The old woman turned to her daughter-in-law. "Oh, Janice, won't you be a dear and pour me a drink?"

Janice hid her irritation, and got up to pour her mother-in-law a drink.

"Really? I have a double—a doppelganger?"

"Your father saw her," Charlotte said.

Georgia sat down next to her grandmother. "Where did you see her, Dad?"

"In an Amish coffee shop of all places. She's a waitress."

"She's Amish?"

"Yes, and a waitress. She makes a good coffee, too, if she was the one who made it."

"You should take Georgia to see her tomorrow, Lyle," Charlotte suggested.

Janice scowled. "Charlotte, Lyle's too busy to do that. We never see him during the day."

"I've got the day off tomorrow. Would you take me, Dad?"

"I could juggle some things around and meet you there at eleven."

"Great, just text me the address and I'll put it into my GPS."

Janice passed her mother-in-law a drink as Georgia left the room.

This was all too close to home; her youngest daughter didn't need to go around looking at people who looked like her. When Janice sat back down on the couch, she wondered if this girl might be the baby she'd given to the Simpsons. She frowned as she tried to remember any clues that they might have joined the Amish. That would certainly explain them refusing the money and closing down that account. It would also explain them selling the house, because they would have had to move closer to other Amish people.

The only thing she could do was go to the coffee shop before Lyle and Georgia. They had mentioned eleven, so that meant that she had to get there before then. She'd know if that was her real daughter.

"Janice!"

She looked across at her husband.

"Where were you? You were a million miles away."

Charlotte had left the room and only Lyle remained.

"Just distracted, sorry. I'm hoping I gave Magda the right menu for dinner."

"She'll sort it out. How was your day?"

"Lyle got another speeding ticket, and they're threatening to throw him out of college again."

"It took me a while to settle into college. Don't worry about him."

"You said you'd take the car away from him if he got another ticket. Are you going to?"

"Okay, but that'll mean you'll have to drive him everywhere."

"Wait until the day after tomorrow, then, if that's okay. I've got some errands to run over the next couple of days. How's Felicity doing?"

Their oldest daughter had just joined the family firm.

"She's doing great. She's got real potential. I've always said that. I think she'll be the one who'll take over my company." He took another sip of his drink.

"What about Lyle?"

He wiggled his mouth. "Not everyone's cut out for it. He'll be successful at something."

"You've always told him he'll take over the company one day."

"No, I haven't. My mother has always told him that. I've been very careful not to say that to him or to anyone else. Anyway, it'll be up to the board of directors."

"How will they feel about a woman taking over, even if she's your daughter?"

"It's ability they'll be looking at. I still think that a woman has to be better than a man to make it in this world, but if anyone's going to do that, it'll be Felicity."

"I always thought you wanted a boy to take over the company. Isn't that why you wanted a son?"

"I never minded whether we had boys or girls."

Janice felt sick to the stomach and the room spun. "I remember you telling me you wanted a son. That's why we were so pleased when Lyle arrived. Lyle the Fourth, to carry on and take over."

"I guess it's nice to have a son but I'd have been just as happy with another girl."

The glass slid out of her fingers and it shattered on the hard marble floor.

"Are you all right?"

"Why are you saying that now? Both you and your mother said how badly you wanted a boy."

He stared at her, speechless at her sudden outburst.

She pulled her gaze away from him. "I have a headache. I need to lie down."

He put his drink down and rushed to her side. "I'll help you."

Once Lyle had helped her to bed, he covered her with blankets.

"Can I get you something?"

"No. It'll pass, it's just one of my migraines. Nothing really works on them."

He leaned down and kissed her softly on her forehead, and quietly left the room. As soon as he was gone, the tears fell down her cheeks. It'd all been for nothing. She loved her son, Lyle, as though he was her own flesh and blood, but that didn't stop her from thinking about her baby girl she gave away. Not a day went by when she wasn't plagued with feelings of guilt and regret. Margaret had been right. She regretted it.

And now...was it all about to blow up in her face just as Margaret had predicted nearly eighteen years ago?

Every day it was clear to her that Lyle didn't fit in with the rest of the family, and if she saw it, what if others did? He was athletic and had a much larger build than the rest of the Doyle men.

If this girl was her daughter, the truth was going to come out and everyone would know the dreadful thing she'd done. How would the two children who'd been swapped react when they learned what had happened? How would her other two daughters react to knowing that the two mothers had deprived them of their sister? And what would they think of her as a mother for doing what she had done? Lyle would divorce her for sure, and she wouldn't be able to blame him.

She had to get a look at this girl before her husband and Georgia got there. When Lyle was in the shower the next morning, Janice would find the message he sent to Georgia regarding the address of the coffee shop and she'd get there to see her before they did.

CHAPTER EIGHT

But the fruit of the Spirit is love, joy, peace, patience, kindness, goodness, faithfulness, gentleness, self-control; against such things there is no law.
Galatians 5:22-23

*a*t nine o'clock the next morning, Janice parked her car across the road from the coffee shop. She was armed with a newspaper so it would look to passersby as though she was doing something. Squinting through the large glass windows, she saw three Amish girls working inside. She'd have to get closer.

The coffee shop was fairly crowded but from where she was, she could see a couple of empty tables. She left her car and walked across the road, pushed the door open, and sat at one of the empty tables.

After she'd been there a minute or two, a woman came to take her order. The woman looked nothing like her daughter. She ordered a coffee and kept looking around for the woman her husband had seen the day before. And then she saw her behind the coffee machine. She could've been Georgia's twin she looked so much like her. The age of the girl looked about right as well. When the girl looked up, Janice put her head down. Janice was suddenly dizzy. She stood up to go get some fresh air, but as soon as she stood she collapsed onto the floor.

Opening her eyes, Janice found herself on her back looking up at the ceiling with a sea of faces looking down at her. When she regained focus, she was looking right into the face of the girl she'd come to see.

"Are you alright?" the girl asked.

Janice couldn't speak. When she heard someone talking about calling 911, she made an effort to raise herself to a sitting position and, as she did so, the girl helped her.

"Are you alright, Ma'am?" the girl asked once more.

Putting her hand to her head, Janice forced herself to say, "Yes."

Someone passed a glass of water to the girl. She offered it to Janice. "Try a sip of water."

Janice took the glass from her and drank a little, sipping slowly. When she'd passed the glass back, she tried to stand.

"Please, Ma'am, stay there for a couple of minutes until you feel better. Do you want me to call someone for you?"

"No! Thank you. I just need a moment." She looked at the girl, seeing eyes that were the same as looking at Felicity and Georgia. This girl was her daughter. There wasn't a doubt in her mind about it. "You're very kind. What's your name?"

"Elizabeth."

"Such a pretty name."

Was her last name Simpson? How would she find out? She took the opportunity, even if the girl thought she was odd for asking. She'd just fainted and everyone had been staring at her so what did it matter if people thought she was odd? "Elizabeth what? What's your last name?"

She took a moment, and then said, "Simpson."

Janice dropped her head into her hands and sobbed. It made things worse when Elizabeth tried to comfort her.

"What can I do for you? Are you sure there's not someone I can call?"

"No." Janice summoned all her strength and pushed herself to her feet as more tears streamed down her face. She leaned over and grabbed her handbag from the table and then headed for the door.

Once she was out of the café, she heard someone behind her.

"Wait! Please, Ma'am, I think you should sit down for a while longer."

It was her daughter.

She whipped her head around. "I'm fine. I need to be somewhere." She walked up the street, not wanting Elizabeth to see what car she got into. When she'd reached the street corner, she turned to see that Elizabeth had gone back inside. Janice then crossed the road and hurried to her car.

ELIZABETH LOOKED out the window as she was placing an order onto a table. The lady who had fainted was now getting into a car. She hoped she was okay to drive, but she'd done all she could to help her.

The day wore on and all Elizabeth could think of was Joseph and whether he might come in on his lunch break. Even though she wasn't able to speak to him much when he had lunch at the café, it was still nice to see him during the day.

"He's back again!" her workmate, Cathy, told her.

"Who is?" She hoped she meant Joseph.

"The man who gave us that large tip, and he has someone with him. Take a look."

Elizabeth had taken over the coffee making and had been behind the coffee machine for the past hour.

"Let's swap. You go out and see him."

Curious, and wondering whether he'd brought his daughter who, he claimed, looked like her, she swapped with her friend and went to take their order.

When she approached the table, she saw a young woman who indeed bore a remarkable resemblance to herself.

The man looked up at her as she approached. "Here she is. I brought you my daughter I was telling you about."

"You do look like me," Elizabeth said, smiling at the young woman.

"Wow! I can't believe it. I really didn't think we'd look that much alike. Where are you from? Have you always lived around here?"

"I moved here when my parents died around ten years ago."

"Oh, I'm sorry to hear that. Were they Amish too?"

Elizabeth shook her head. "No. Do you live close?"

"Not that far. About an hour away," the man said.

"What can I get for you today?" Elizabeth asked, not at all comfortable talking about herself with strangers.

Once they placed their order, Elizabeth hurried away. She wondered if the girl might be some relation, maybe a distant relative. Perhaps she should look further into her parents' records to see if they had at least one living relative. Since she'd lived amongst the Amish with all the uncles, aunts, and cousins everyone was surrounded with, it was hard to believe that two people could have had no relations at all.

As she waited for the coffees to be made, she decided that she would see if they wanted to exchange addresses and phone numbers in case there was some connection that existed. She scribbled down her address and the Grabers' phone number on a nearby slip of paper. When the coffees were ready, she picked them up and headed back to the table with the slip of paper wedged between her fingers.

"Would you like to exchange addresses and phone numbers? I'm going to search and see if my parents had some relatives. We might be related somehow."

"I don't know if we are, but sure." The young woman looked into her bag. "Do you have a piece of paper?"

Elizabeth ripped the paper she'd given them in half. "You can use this. I'm Elizabeth by the way. Elizabeth Simpson."

The girl looked up from writing down her details. "And I'm Georgia Doyle, and this is my father, Lyle Doyle."

She nodded and smiled at the older man, now knowing that his story had been true and that he hadn't had any bad intentions.

When Mr. Doyle and his daughter finally left the coffee shop, Elizabeth couldn't help the weird sensation looming over her. They were obviously rich because the man had left another huge tip. The woman from earlier that morning had gotten into a very expensive car, not a type normally seen in that part of town, and she had asked her last name, becoming even more distressed at the Simpson name. Could there be a connection between that lady and these two people? It made her more determined to look into her family's history.

CHAPTER NINE

The Lord is slow to anger and great in power,
and the Lord will by no means clear the guilty.
His way is in whirlwind and storm,
and the clouds are the dust of his feet.
Nahum 1:3

*J*anice went straight home and lay down in a darkened room with ice chips rolled into a towel and placed across her forehead. Her fainting spell had now developed into a bad headache. It was only two weeks away from Elizabeth's birthday, which was Christmas day, the same as young Lyle's, the day that she had chosen to swap her for a stranger's son. A wave of nausea swept over her and she leaned over the bed and heaved.

Her housekeeper walked into her room. "Are you okay?"

"No. I'm sick."

"Can I get you anything?"

"No."

She came closer and saw the vomit on the floor. "I'll clean that up."

Janice turned around and buried her head in the pillow. As much as she loved her son, Lyle, she wished she could turn back time. She never would've made the stupid swap. Tossing and turning for the next few hours, she couldn't help but wonder what would happen next. How did Elizabeth and her parents end up with the Amish?

She dozed off and the next thing she knew someone sat on the bed beside her. When she smelled her husband's aftershave, she closed her eyes and didn't turn around. If he thought she was asleep, he'd leave her be. Magda would've told him she wasn't feeling well. The last thing she wanted was for him to tell her about seeing Elizabeth again.

When she woke the next morning, she heard her husband's shower running. She pulled on a bathrobe and went downstairs. Their housekeeper was in the kitchen preparing breakfast.

"Coffee or tea, Mrs. Doyle?"

"Yes please."

"Which one this morning?"

"Oh, tea please."

"You feeling a lot better?"

"Yes." She sat down and pretended to be interested in the day's newspaper that was on the table in front of her.

ELIZABETH WOKE up pleased to have a day off. She'd arranged to meet Joseph briefly in town over his lunch break. She walked into the kitchen where Tara and Megan were already eating breakfast.

"Why are you looking so happy?" Tara asked as Elizabeth sat down.

"I'm seeing Joseph later today."

"I wish I had a man who made me smile like that."

Megan said, "You've got your choice of men, don't you?"

"I don't like any of them that much. I don't like any of them enough to marry them or anything." She gave a giggle and added, "Not like Elizabeth loves Joseph."

Elizabeth kept quiet, wanting to keep her feelings for him to herself, betrayed only by the small smile she couldn't keep from her lips.

Mrs. Graber put a pile of pancakes in the center of the table. "Don't you girls have anything to talk about other than men?"

"Nee," said Tara, causing the other two girls to giggle.

"I've got something else to talk about." Elizabeth placed two pancakes on her plate.

"What is it?" Mrs. Graber asked as she joined them.

"Yesterday I saw a girl who looked exactly like me. Well, not exactly but very much like me."

"Where was that?" Gretchen Graber asked.

"It was in the coffee shop. Her father had been in the day before and he told me that his daughter looked like me. I thought nothing of it until he brought his daughter back the next day."

"Who were these people?" Tara asked.

"I don't remember the last name, but her first name was Georgia and they said they live about an hour away."

Tara's eyes opened wide. "Are you related possibly?"

"I was told my parents had no relations." She looked at Gretchen. "Is that right?"

"That's what they told me, and that's all I know."

"How would I find out for certain?"

Aunt Gretchen shook her head. "I'm not certain. I could give you the phone number of the social worker."

"Okay. I'd like to find out if I do have some relations. It seems that everyone's got someone, unless my parents were both orphans or something."

"Oh, now I'm keen to know if this girl is related to you. Was she older or younger?" Tara asked.

"I don't know. Possibly the same age or maybe a little older; I don't think she was younger from what I could tell."

"Surely you could get your birth records and trace your parents that way."

"I guess so. I'll look into it. The girl and I exchanged phone numbers and addresses." Elizabeth cut a slice of pancake and placed it into her mouth.

JANICE FELT her body stiffen when her husband walked into the breakfast room.

He stared at her. "You better?"

"Yes. It was just another migraine."

"You should go back to the doctor about that. You get them too frequently."

"There's not much they can do about them."

"I'm not so sure about that." He sat down at the table without kissing her good morning as he normally would've.

"Have you finished with the paper?"

She pushed it over to him.

"Thanks."

Magda placed Lyle's usual mug of coffee in front of him. He took a mouthful while he read the paper. He'd never done that before. Normally they had a conversation which he'd start by asking her what she was going to do that day. Had Elizabeth told him something about herself? Did he know something he was keeping from her?

She had to know. After she took a deep breath, she asked, "How did your trip with Georgia go yesterday?"

He raised his eyebrows and looked over at her. "Good. Georgia saw the girl and they exchanged numbers. The girl is looking into her parents' family tree. Maybe she's some distant relation to us. She thinks she has no living relatives. Her parents died, and now she's living with an Amish family.

"They died?"

He frowned at her. "Yes. It's sad. She said they died some years ago."

"That's awful. How did they die?"

"She didn't say. I'm surprised she told us that much." He went back to reading his paper.

"Yes. That's true."

"Here's your tea, Mrs. Doyle. Can I get you anything besides toast? Anything for the headache?"

Every morning, Janice had two slices of toast with marmalade.

"Just the toast thanks. I'm fine. The headache's gone now. And thanks for cleaning up last night."

The housekeeper gave her a nod.

"We'll have all the children home again soon," Lyle said.

"What do you mean?" Janice asked.

"Lyle's coming back from college. We'll have the three of them here for a big family Christmas."

There was a weird tension between them. Janice could feel it. They'd always had their three children there for Christmas, so why had he said that? Was he suspicious? Lyle Junior had grown to six feet two, when all the Doyle men were no more than five eight. He was also not as good academically as the rest of their family.

She swallowed a mouthful of tea far too quickly and burned her mouth causing her to crash the cup back onto the saucer. Her fingertips flew to her mouth as the hot liquid scalded the back of her throat.

"Are you sure you're okay?"

"I might lie down again."

"That's it. I'm calling the doctor," Lyle said.

"No! Please don't. I'll be fine. I just need to rest. Magda, can you bring my toast up to me?"

"Yes, Mrs. Doyle."

Janice left the room quickly, unable to sit in the same room as her husband.

A few moments later, Magda brought her toast to her. "Mr. Doyle's left and he said he'd call you to check on you later."

"Thank you, Magda."

After her housekeeper left the room, Janice had to talk to someone. She called the only other person who knew about the swap, her midwife and good friend, Margaret.

CHAPTER TEN

The Lord is slow to anger and abounding in steadfast love,
forgiving iniquity and transgression,
but he will by no means clear the guilty,
visiting the iniquity of the fathers on the children,
to the third and the fourth generation
Numbers 14:18

*M*argaret answered the phone as though she was half asleep.

"Did I wake you?"

"Janice?"

"Yes."

"Is everything okay?"

"I don't know. Do you have time to talk?"

"I guess so. I'm awake now. I only got to sleep at two, I was working."

"I'm sorry."

"That's all right. What's going on?"

"I don't know where to start." She took a deep breath. "I think Lyle has found the baby I swapped."

"How? What do you mean?"

"He went to a coffee shop somewhere and came home and told me about this girl who looked like Georgia. I didn't think much of it, but then I got worried when he arranged for Georgia to go back with him to see the girl the next day."

"Do you think it's her?"

"I didn't at first. But I went there myself yesterday morning, before they went there. She looks very much like Georgia and a little like Felicity."

Margaret was silent.

"Lyle came back and told me that the girl said her parents died awhile back, and she has no relatives. She was taken in by an Amish family. She's wearing Amish clothes and she speaks differently than us."

Janice fought back tears. When she was met with silence on the other end of the phone, she knew that Margaret was stopping herself from saying, *I told you this would blow up in our faces!* "Margaret, are you still there?"

"I don't know what to say."

"I think Lyle might know. He was acting weird this morning."

"He couldn't possibly know. It's just your guilty conscience making you feel that. He couldn't possibly have figured it out."

"You don't think so?"

"No. I don't!"

"What about how Lyle Junior looks so different?"

"That's not unusual. Your father was very tall, too, don't forget."

"I guess so. What am I going to do?"

"Nothing. There's nothing you can do. Just forget it. There's no way anyone can find out. Their birth certificates show that Lyle is yours and the other baby was the other couples. DNA tests are the only thing that would say otherwise. Don't worry. You can't lose your nerve—for both our sakes."

"Okay." Janice sniffed.

"Just keep away from the girl and it'll all blow over."

"Do you think so?"

"Yes."

"Thanks. I feel better."

"Good. Now pull yourself together and call me later."

When Janice ended her conversation with Margaret she felt much better. If it weren't Christmas time, she could've visited some friends and gotten away for a while. It just wasn't possible to be away from her family in the holidays. She'd have to keep it together, just as Margaret had said.

LATER THAT DAY, Janice drove past the same coffee shop. She wanted to get another glimpse of her daughter. There was no sign of her in the café, she realized after she'd driven past four times. When Janice headed home, she remembered how her daughter had been so kind to her; Janice was pleased that she'd grown into a kind and caring person. How desperately she hoped that her daughter was happy and had a good life.

As SHE SAT down at the dinner table that night with her two daughters and her husband, Janice put on a brave face. Lyle had again been behaving strangely toward her since he'd arrived home.

Tonight she didn't mind that her older daughter and her husband discussed business.

When there was a lull in their conversation, Georgia said to her sister, "Did you hear about the girl we saw in the coffee shop yesterday?"

"Yes. Dad told me. You should've taken a photo with her."

"What girl?" their grandmother asked.

"A girl who looked exactly like me," Georgia explained. "You should've come with us, Granny."

"Oh, that girl. Well, I would've if I'd been asked. As usual, no one includes me in anything."

Georgia ignored her grandmother's comment. "She's an Amish girl."

"I don't know if she was properly Amish. She said she was taken in by them," Lyle said.

Georgia played with her food. "Well, she was wearing the clothing."

"How much did she look like you, Georgia?" Charlotte asked.

"They say everyone has a double," Janice said. "When I arrived at college many years ago, everyone told me there was another girl who looked exactly like me. When I eventually saw her, I didn't think she looked anything like me." Janice glanced up at her husband to see his eyes fixed on hers. She gave him a little smile before she looked back down at her food.

"I'd like to go and see her," Charlotte said.

Janice said, "Nonsense. The poor girl will feel like she's on display. Leave her be."

Charlotte glared at her daughter-in-law. "How are you feeling now, Janice?"

"Fine."

"I really think you should see a doctor about these constant headaches," Lyle said.

Felicity nodded in agreement. "Yeah, Mom. It could be something serious."

"It's fine. I've been tested for other things and they found nothing. They're just brought on by stress."

"What are you stressed about, dear?" Charlotte asked her. "You have everything you want. You don't have to lift a finger around this place."

Georgia answered, "Lyle of course, Granny. Everyone's stressed about him. Didn't you hear about the car accident he had yesterday? He totaled the car."

"He had an accident?" Janice asked. "Is he hurt?"

"He's fine, but the car isn't. Georgia, we were keeping that from your mother, remember?"

"What about all the other things he does? You'd never let Felicity or me get away with all the things he does. You should be stricter with him. You and Mom let him get away with everything."

"Where's the car now?" Janice asked.

Lyle shook his head. "Don't worry. It's all been taken care of. I think he needs to have some consequences for his behavior."

"Yes, well, think of a way to punish him," Janice said.

"Finally!" Felicity looked over at Georgia who nodded in agreement.

Janice was pleased that the conversation had gotten away from Elizabeth.

DAYS LATER, Janice's husband came home early and sat down in front of her when she was watching TV. Charlotte was in her bedroom having a nap, their daughters were out and, apart from their housekeeper, they had the place to themselves.

Janice stared at Lyle, wondering what was on his mind. "What is it?"

"You've been acting a little odd lately."

She frowned at him. "That's what I've been thinking about you. You've been distant."

He narrowed his eyes and tipped his head to one side. "Is there anything you want to tell me?"

"Like?"

"Anything at all?"

She shook her head. "I can't think of anything."

"I had someone check into a few things for me."

"Is that about buying Lyle that new car? Because I used my own money."

"It's not about the car," he said shaking his head. "There are far more important things going on."

"What is it? Just tell me."

"I had someone look into some things, as I said, and there was another child born in Margaret's birthing center on the same day. They had a girl, and that girl was Elizabeth—the girl who strikingly resembles Georgia."

He knows!

She opened her mouth, and no words came out. She wanted to make some kind of excuse to put his fears at rest, but she had no excuse.

"What I want to know is whether that girl is my daughter." He stared at her.

CHAPTER ELEVEN

Blessed is the man that walketh not in the counsel of the ungodly, nor standeth in the way of sinners, nor sitteth in the seat of the scornful.
Psalms 1:1

*T*he truth was going to come out eventually. There was no use hiding it any longer.

She stared down at the soft colored patterns on the Persian carpet under her feet, unable to look him in his eyes. "We swapped babies."

When she heard him gasp, she looked up at him to see his head jerk backward and his eyes open wide in disbelief.

"You wanted a boy," she blurted in her defense.

He lifted his hand in the air. "Wait! You did what?"

"I thought you knew."

There was silence before he spoke again. "All I had were suspicions, but what you've just said… I don't believe you could do such a thing." He held both sides of his head. "I feel like I'm having a bad dream. This can't be real."

"Everyone wanted a boy. I couldn't take the pressure."

"There was never any pressure." He shook his head at her and then drew his eyes away as though he could no longer bear to look at her.

"Yes there was, horrible pressure from your mother. She's spiteful and always telling me I'm no good. I'm sorry. I've never said anything bad about her to you before, but you must see how she is."

"You gave our baby away, Janice! Our own baby! How could you do that?" He put both hands to his face and rubbed hard.

"I took in their baby and they took mine."

"Not yours, Janice, ours. You gave her away. How could you?" He jumped to his feet. Before long, he was pacing up and down in front of her with a hand on his forehead and his cheeks beet red, looking as though he would explode.

"I know it was a terrible thing to do and I can't live with the guilt anymore." Now that the truth had come out, it was a relief. Even if Lyle divorced her, she thought, she would've died if she'd had to keep the secret any longer. "You can divorce me. I won't fight it."

Once he finished pacing, he sat opposite her. "I don't know how you could possibly give away our child."

"I did it for us. I knew you'd divorce me if I didn't give you a son."

He scoffed. "We're not in the dark ages. I don't need a son. I don't have a throne and a kingdom."

In a small voice she said, "You wanted one, though. You said it a number of times."

"It didn't matter to me—boy or girl. Does Margaret know of this? I suppose she would've had to have been in on it."

"I made her keep quiet."

"Is that because she borrowed all that money from you for her birthing center?"

"I guess that helped."

He shook his head and leaned back in the couch. Suddenly, he sprang forward. "How did you get the other couple to agree with the madness?"

"They were poor. I gave them a large sum up front, and then monthly payments. Years ago, the automatic deposits suddenly stopped going through."

"Our daughter went into the foster care system. What do you think about that? Why didn't you look into things when the payments stopped?"

"I did. I tried. I went to their house, but it was sold. The realtor wouldn't give me any information and neither would their bank. What was I to do? I thought they might suddenly have decided not to take the money anymore. I didn't know they'd died. I didn't know!" When she thought of her small daughter all alone with strangers—the love of a mother and father gone—she put both hands up to her face and cried. "I didn't know she was in foster care. How could I know? Every time I thought of her it was with loving parents who cared for her."

"Stop it, Janice. What's done is done. We can't go back. All we can do is figure out how to make this messy situation work. The truth has to come out. That's the only way."

Sniffing back her tears, she asked him, "You're not going to divorce me?"

He frowned. "I don't know. No. I didn't marry to get a divorce. I married for life. I'll calm down. I can't believe what you've done, but this family needs you. We'll sort things out, and we'll make this work. The truth needs to come out."

"Does it?"

"There's no way around it."

"How will Lyle feel, and what about Georgia and Felicity? Oh, and I don't want your mother to know."

"I know mother is hard to get along with and she'll have a lot to say about it. Ignore her."

"What about Lyle?"

"What about Elizabeth? She's the one who's been the most damaged. She's been from one house to another. I found out the Amish family wasn't the first one she was placed with."

"Don't make me feel worse than I already do."

"We have to make this right."

She sighed. "How?"

"You and I will have to tell her, and tell the family she's living with."

Janice's stomach churned at the thought. Then her thoughts turned to Lyle. "Lyle's coming home for dinner tonight."

"Good. We'll tell him tonight and tomorrow we'll go to Elizabeth's house."

"You've got her address?"

"She gave Georgia her address. I had a private investigator look into things. That's how I found all this out. The first time I was at the coffee shop, I found out her name and…"

"You were suspicious back then?"

"I wasn't, not until I saw your reaction to hearing about her. I know you better than you realize."

It was true. When he was away on business trips and she tried to hide that she was ill, he always knew just by the sound of her voice.

"I'm sorry, Lyle. I've made a mess of things."

"Yes, there's no doubt you have. Whenever something goes wrong in the company, we focus on fixing it. That's what we have to do here."

She sniffled. "You're not going to divorce me?"

He shrugged. "Why do you keep saying that?"

"Most of our friends are divorced, and their wives wouldn't have done anything as horrible as this."

"I've already told you I've no intention of ever getting a divorce. Right now we have to sort this out the best we can. We have to visit Elizabeth and her foster family."

THAT NIGHT when they told Lyle Junior the truth of everything, he took the news well.

"That explains a lot."

"Lyle, can you ever forgive me?" Janice asked.

He stood up, leaned over and hugged his mother. "I must've been some handsome baby."

She gave a laugh. "You were. I'm so sorry, though, that you never got to meet your birth parents."

He stepped back. "There's nothing to forgive." He scratched his head. "It makes me feel a little odd, though. I thought I knew who I was and now I'm not one of you. It feels a little weird. It'll take some getting used to."

"You are one of us," his father said.

"You are my parents. You were the ones who raised me. I wouldn't mind finding out about the couple who gave birth to me. I wish they were still around. I wonder if my birth father was into sports. I can find all that out from Elizabeth."

Lyle Senior said, "We're going to have to break the news to your sisters tonight and then go and talk to Elizabeth and her family tomorrow."

"How do you think she'll take it?" Lyle Junior asked.

He shook his head. "I don't know."

Janice studied Lyle Junior's face. His words showed that he was taking the news well, but something like this would have to rock him to the core. "I think we should all go to family counseling about this."

"That won't be necessary, Mom."

"I think it's important that we all go; your sisters as well."

"Your mother's right, Lyle. The hard thing will be for us all to make the time to go."

"Does Granny know all this?"

"No, she doesn't. We're delaying telling her for as long as we can," Janice said knowing that her mother-in-law would be none too pleased.

"I'm happy you two raised me. I'm glad I'm here. I couldn't have had a better life."

Janice stepped forward and gave him a hug. Something told her not everyone else would take the news as well as he.

CHAPTER TWELVE

Therefore I say unto you, What things soever ye desire,
when ye pray, believe that ye receive them,
and ye shall have them.
Mark 11:24

*J*anice knew this was something she had to do. She'd made a mistake and now she had to go through the shame and embarrassment to repair what she'd done.

Lyle and Janice drove to Elizabeth's house in silence. Even though Elizabeth had given Georgia her phone number, Lyle chose not to call first. There was no way he could've explained over the phone what he wanted to speak with them about.

When they pulled up outside the white farmhouse, Janice grabbed her husband's arm. "Shouldn't we be doing this with the help of a social worker or something?"

"I don't see why. We're just telling them the truth."

Now there was no going back. A woman in her mid-fifties was looking out the window at them.

They walked to the front door and before they reached it, the woman opened the door. She was a plain looking woman with not a lick of make up. Her salt-and-pepper hair was severely pulled back off her face, most of it hidden under a white cap. Her ruddy cheeks grew wider as she smiled and her pale blue eyes crinkled at the corners.

"Hello," she said.

Lyle glanced at his wife and then back at the woman. "Hello, are you Mrs. Graber?"

"I am."

"We're here to talk with you and your husband about Elizabeth. Would she be home at the moment?"

"She's at work."

"Could we request a bit of your time?" Janice asked.

The woman stepped aside to allow them in.

Once they were seated, Janice confessed the whole story in between bouts of sobbing with her face buried in tissues. "Oh, I didn't want to cry."

Lyle put a comforting hand on Janice's shoulder.

Mr. Graber, a man with a long gray and brown beard, walked through the door and his wife conveyed the story to him. After that, Mr. Graber sat down with them.

Janice looked at the Amish couple seated on the couch in front of her. "I suppose you think I'm a dreadful person."

Mr. Graber shook his head. "We don't judge."

"God wanted Elizabeth here and that's why she's here," Mrs. Graber said matter-of-factly.

"Thank you for looking after her. You seem to be really nice people. We heard she was somewhere else before she came here. Was she okay there?"

Mrs. Graber answered, "She was briefly with two families, but they weren't able to give her a permanent home. I think she was okay. Nothing bad happened to her, if that's what you mean."

"Yes. Good. That's good." Janice glanced at her husband.

"Elizabeth will be home soon if you want to tell her yourselves. She's old enough to choose where she wants to go now that she's... Oh wait. She won't be eighteen until the twenty fifth."

"It's the other two girls who are over eighteen," Mr. Graber told his wife.

"You have other foster children?" Lyle asked.

"When we couldn't have our own, we knew God had a plan. We're all God's children, and now God has been able to use us to help in the broader community."

"You're wonderful people for giving them a home." Janice knew that they were loving as soon as she walked in; she could feel the peace and the love in the house. Her daughter had been fortunate, but things could have been very different and she'd only have herself to blame if Elizabeth had suffered in any way.

"We can't thank you enough for looking after her," Lyle said.

"So, will she stay on after her birthday? You said the other foster children are now older than eighteen," Janice asked.

"She can make her choice. Tara and Megan have chosen to live on here, but they're free to go at anytime."

"Have they become Amish?" Lyle asked.

"They haven't been baptized yet, but our job has been to care for them not to force them to join us."

Lyle rubbed his hands together. "Of course not. I didn't mean to imply that you were recruiting people into your faith or anything like that."

"God chooses people to come to us and then they are free to make their decision when they are older," Mrs. Graber said.

"How do you think Elizabeth will take the news?"

"I don't know," she said, turning to her husband. "What do you think?"

He shook his head. "She's a calm and pleasant girl with compassion and understanding."

His words gave Janice hope. Hope that Elizabeth would forgive her for the dreadful thing she'd done. Lyle Junior had appeared to take it well, but she was certain that he'd have questions as he processed the whole situation.

ELIZABETH FINISHED work and Joseph met her to give her a ride home.

"How was your day?" he asked when she climbed into the buggy beside him.

"Busy!"

He checked for cars behind him and then clicked his horse forward. "No more visits from people who look like you?"

She laughed. "No. That was weird."

"I've got my skates in the back if you want to go skating."

Elizabeth slapped him playfully on the arm. "Why didn't you tell me? I've left mine at home. I didn't think to bring them."

"I thought you'd bring them with you. Aren't you keen to give me more lessons?"

"I've gone as far as I can go with them. The rest is only practice."

"Where will we go? I can't take you home now."

"If I go home to get my skates, I can't really go out again. Aunt Gretchen will expect me to stay home and help her with dinner or something."

"You could watch me skate."

"Watching you fall over all the time is no fun. And you hurt my ears when you crash-land on the ice."

He laughed. "I'm not that bad am I?"

She nodded. "You know you are."

"You told me I was getting better."

"You are, but you were so bad before that it's not much of a compliment."

He frowned at her. "Well, I'm not taking you straight home. We'll go for a long drive."

She giggled.

After some time, Joseph stopped the buggy at the side of a quiet road.

"Have you done anything about finding relatives?"

"Not yet. I'm going to contact one of the social workers Gretchen knows and see if she can point me in the right direction. I think that's the simplest way to go."

"Good idea. Are you going to stay on in the community once you turn eighteen?"

"That's the thing I don't know. I've thought about leaving, but it's a little scary."

"You'd soon make friends and you don't strike me as someone who couldn't make her own way. You already have a job, so that's a good start."

"Joseph, are you trying to talk me into leaving?"

He smiled and took hold of her hand. "I want you to stay, and fall in love with me, and marry me."

She smiled and pulled her hand away. It was hard to know when he was being serious. Or maybe his joking manner gave him the courage to speak what was in his heart.

"I know you must make your own decision. I'm just saying that if you stay on, I'll be happy."

"You just want free skating lessons."

"Why wouldn't I? That's all I want you to stay for."

She slapped him on his shoulder and he tried to duck out of her way.

"Do you get two presents or one present for your birthday since it's on Christmas Day?"

She stared at him. "Where did that come from?"

His eyes sparkled as his lips turned upward. "It's a problem I've been thinking about."

"If it's that much of a problem, you should give me two."

He pulled away from her and frowned. "Who said I was getting you anything? All I said was, 'Do you get two presents or one?' I never said I was getting you anything. I didn't give you anything last year."

"We didn't know each other last year."

"See?"

She shook her head. "You always have to be right."

He wagged his finger at her. "I *am* always right. I'm glad you agree."

"You're impossible."

"Impossibly smart, and impossibly handsome."

She grunted at him and shook her head again. "Now that you're getting me a present, I suppose I'll have to get you a small something."

"Small? That doesn't sound very good."

Elizabeth laughed. "Depends what it is!"

"What do you have in mind?"

"Nothing yet. You'll have to wait and see."

"Does that mean we'll see each other on Christmas Day?"

"Would you like to?"

He nodded. "You know I would."

"Would your folks mind if you came over for the evening meal on Christmas Day?"

"I've got nine brothers, and seven of them will have their wives and families there, so I don't think they'll miss me."

"That's a big family."

"Yeah."

"Good. I'll let Aunt Gretchen know that you'll be there."

He fidgeted with the reins. "Are you sure it'll be okay?"

"Why wouldn't it be?"

"This is a serious step in our relationship."

"Christmas dinner is a serious step?"

He grinned cheekily. "Very serious."

She looked out of the buggy. "We should go. Aunt Gretchen will be wondering where I am. I don't want to worry her."

CHAPTER THIRTEEN

But my God shall supply all your need
according to his riches in glory by Christ Jesus.
Philippians 4:19

*E*lizabeth stepped out of Joseph's buggy when he stopped his horse outside her house. "Will I see you tomorrow?"

"You can count on it." He gave her a little wink before he turned the buggy around.

As she raced toward her front door, she noticed a car parked by the barn. She thought it must be one of the caseworkers the Grabers regularly saw.

She opened the front door and stepped into the warmth of the house. As she was taking off her coat, Aunt Gretchen hurried toward her.

"There are people here to see you."

"Who?"

"Come." Aunt Gretchen took hold of her arm and walked her into the living room.

There she saw the man from the coffee shop, and he was with the woman who had fainted at the shop. She stared curiously at the two of them, waiting for someone to speak.

"You should sit down."

When she heard Uncle William's voice, she noticed that he was also in the room. She sat down, took a deep breath, and waited to learn why they were there.

The woman cleared her throat. "I should be the one to tell her."

"Tell me what?" She hoped she wasn't in trouble for something.

The man nodded.

Elizabeth sat stiffly as she listened to the outrageous tale.

The woman told her that she'd been swapped at birth for a boy and they were her real parents and not the Simpsons who had raised her. They had raised the Simpsons' boy as their own. The man took over and explained that they hadn't known that the Simpsons had died. The woman had paid the Simpsons money, and then the deposits had just stopped going into the Simpsons account, with no explanation.

"I don't believe it! The Simpsons were my parents! This can't be true!"

"They were but they weren't, Elizabeth," the man insisted. "I'm afraid it's all true. Everything my wife has said."

"They pretended to be my parents... were my parents for money?"

"No, Elizabeth. It wasn't like that. They loved you and raised you as their own. I offered them money to help them out."

"It wasn't to help them. You wanted a boy and not a girl. You didn't want me!"

The woman bowed her head.

"You should be ashamed," Elizabeth spat out, finding anger within that she'd never before experienced. "Where is my mother and father's real child—the boy?"

"We've raised him," the man explained.

"Does he know all this?"

"We told him yesterday," Mr. Doyle said.

"Don't blame your father. He's only just learned of this since he saw you in the coffee shop," Mrs. Doyle said.

Elizabeth sprang to her feet and yelled, "He is *not* my father!"

"I think you should listen to them, Elizabeth."

Calmed by Uncle William's words, she sat down again. She looked from Mr. Doyle to Mrs. Doyle, waiting for one of them to say something. Aunt Gretchen was now sitting beside her, speechless. She glanced at Aunt Gretchen to see a worry-lined face.

"We thought you should know the truth," Mr. Doyle said.

"Good. Great! Now I know that my parents weren't my parents and they raised me for money. I also know that my birth mother gave me away to strangers without a second thought, preferring some stranger's baby to me."

"It wasn't like that," Mrs. Doyle said in a small voice.

"Explain to me what it was like, then," Elizabeth demanded.

Mrs. Doyle shook her head and cried while her husband put his arm around her.

"This is the way she explained it to me, as weird as it's going to sound. My wife felt pressured to have a boy. She thought I'd only be happy with a boy and thought I'd divorce her and marry someone else and try for a boy if she couldn't give me one. I wasn't at your birth like I was at the births of our other daughters. I couldn't get back in time because of bad weather. The airports were closed. I had to wait and then hire a car and drive back home. She saw an opportunity when another couple had a boy. They were poor, and Elizabeth offered them money. The midwife knew they were good people otherwise my wife never would have swapped babies if she wasn't certain you'd have a good life, and that is the reason she sent them money to ensure you'd never go without."

"Well, I did go without. They died."

"I'm sorry," Mrs. Doyle said.

"All this time I thought they were my real parents. They lied to me every single day of my life."

"It wasn't a lie. You were their child just as Lyle is our child and always will be."

"There's truth in what the man says, Elizabeth," Mr. Graber said. "We love all our children and none of you were born to us."

Elizabeth closed her eyes and tried to absorb all that she'd been told. Her past, her whole past had been a lie. Events had led her to be with the Grabers who had been her mom and dad for the past ten years.

"This lady, and this man here, they are my real parents because they would never lie to me." Elizabeth pointed to the Grabers as she spoke.

"We're not trying to take anything away from anyone, Elizabeth. We've come here risking that you'll hate us, or not accept us. We just want you to finally know the truth of where you came from. We want the truth to be out once and for all," Mr. Doyle said.

She glanced over at Mrs. Doyle who was still hanging her head in shame. It couldn't have been easy for her to admit what she'd done.

"I can appreciate you coming forward with the truth. I guess it wouldn't have been an easy thing to do," Elizabeth said, now appreciating the life she had with the Grabers more deeply. They would never lie to her about anything.

"We should go, but we'd like to see you again, Elizabeth. And maybe you might like to meet the rest of your family. You have two sisters, and your brother, the Simpson's son. He's keen to ask you about his birth parents."

Elizabeth swallowed her words about them not being her family. "I'd like to meet him and tell him about them. What I remember of them anyway." Now looking at her birth mother with tear-filled eyes, she asked, "Did you ever miss me?"

"Every day. I thought of you every day. I cried all the time at first; I missed you and wanted to hold you. I had another baby to love and care for. When I craved to hold you, I cuddled him. Your mother and I each had a baby to love and we did. All I can do is say that I'm truly, truly sorry for what I've done to you and to all of us."

Mr. Doyle tapped his wife on her shoulder as he stood up. She stood as well and so did the Grabers. Elizabeth stayed seated, fearing she'd fall if she stood. They said goodbye to her and she nodded when they said they'd leave all their phone numbers with the Grabers.

When they left, Mrs. Graber went to put the dinner on while Mr. Graber sat down with her.

"How are you feeling?"

"I'm in shock. My parents weren't my parents. I was sold."

"Gott has his hand on you. You've come to us for a reason. Don't take anger out on these people. They've

admitted their wrongdoing and they've confessed everything. It took courage for them to tell you."

"I know. I saw the look on her face. It was hard for her. It was such a horrible thing to do."

"There's an old saying, Elizabeth, that you shouldn't judge others until you've walked a mile in their shoes. You don't know the woman's state in her head at the time. She's had to live with that mistake and keep it hidden for nearly eighteen years."

Elizabeth nodded in acknowledgment of the truth in what he was saying, but she was far more concerned about herself than how it had affected the woman who'd given her up.

"Don't forget, you're here because this is where *Gott* wanted you. If Mrs. Doyle hadn't made that choice, you wouldn't be here."

"I couldn't imagine not being here. I love it here. This is my home." Now more than she ever had before, Elizabeth knew she belonged with the Amish. They were gentle and caring people and they never would have made silly reckless choices like her birth mother had made. "I suppose I take after that woman. I hope I don't make bad choices."

"You won't. You're the most sensible girl I know."

She looked at the kind old man she'd resisted calling *Dat* in memory of the man she had thought was her father. The Simpsons who had raised her had looked after her well, but now she questioned their motivations. "Can I call you *Dat?*"

He laughed. "I told you when you first arrived here; you can call me whatever you like, just don't call me late for dinner."

Smiling at the old joke she'd heard so many times before, she moved next to him and gave him a hug. "Thanks, *Dat*."

CHAPTER FOURTEEN

God is not a man, that he should lie;
neither the son of man, that he should repent:
hath he said, and shall he not do it?
or hath he spoken, and shall he not make it good?
Numbers 23:19

"*T*hat went badly," Janice said to her husband when they drove away.

"I expected it to. She was hardly going to welcome us with open arms. Let her get used to the idea and one day she might come around to not hating us."

"It's me she should hate, not you."

"At least we know she's been loved and cared for. They were such lovely people."

Janice remained silent while she dealt with feelings of jealousy that her daughter cared so much for the Grabers and was now calling them her real parents.

Lyle gripped the steering wheel so hard his knuckles were white. "It's all such a mess. I don't know how my mother will take it. It'll probably kill her."

"At least something good might come out of it, then." The words had slipped out of Janice's mouth before she could stop them.

Lyle took his eyes off the road to glare at his wife.

"I'm sorry, Lyle. I didn't mean it. I'm just stressed; I don't know what I'm saying."

He frowned and turned his concentration back to the road ahead.

Janice stared at her husband. "Is there a way around telling her?"

"No. Once the girls know, she'll find out; and you know Lyle's never been able to keep anything quiet."

"Is it true you didn't care whether you had a boy or a girl?"

"I told you. It didn't matter. It was nice to have a boy, but I would've loved a girl just as much. It never mattered. I'm sorry you felt so pressured." He glanced at her. "Don't be upset. This whole thing must've been so hard on you, keeping this buried all these years."

"It has. It's been dreadful. Every time I heard the doorbell buzz, I feared it would be the Simpsons exposing the secret. I thought about her every day."

"You did it all for me?"

"To be truthful, I did it because I wanted to keep you happy so you wouldn't divorce me."

He frowned at her. "I wouldn't divorce you. Mind you, it crossed my mind when all this first came out. I didn't get married to divorce; I meant my vows."

"You've always been faithful?"

"Of course, I have."

"What about all those business trips?"

He shook his head. "When I go away, I spend half the time at night on the phone to you. I'd hardly get the time. I've always been faithful to you. As faithful as a pair of old slippers." He chuckled. "It's me who should be fearful of you divorcing me."

"Why would I even think about it?"

"I'm old and cranky, and you always tell me I work too much. And I brought my mother to live with us."

"That's all true, but divorcing you never crossed my mind."

"Next year, I'm cutting back on my work. Now that the children are grown, we should spend more time together. We'll travel."

"Really?"

"Why not? Let's enjoy life."

"I'll only be able to enjoy life if Elizabeth forgives me. If one of our other children were angry with us, I'd bribe them with something like a car, but we can't do that with Elizabeth. Not now that she's been so many years with the Amish."

"This situation has forced us to take a good look at ourselves and our life."

She nodded and looked at the road ahead, hoping all their lives would change for the better.

WHEN ELIZABETH HEARD Tara and Megan come home, she said, "I must go and tell them what happened."

William nodded.

She hurried out the door pulling her shawl around her shoulders. When she got to the barn, Tara and Megan were climbing down from the buggy.

Tara immediately looked at her. "What's wrong?"

"I don't know where to start. Something's happened."

"Are *Mamm* and *Dat* okay?" Megan asked, rushing at her.

"*Jah*, it's not about them, it's about me. Remember I told you all about the man with the daughter who looked like me?"

"*Jah.*"

"They were here—him and his wife. They say I'm their daughter. They swapped me at birth for a boy."

"But your parents died in the car accident," Megan said.

"They're saying that they are my real parents, and the people who died are the ones who took me when they gave up their son."

"Who would do such a thing?" Megan asked.

Elizabeth breathed out heavily feeling better now that she'd told her two best friends. "That girl was my sister and there's another sister, an older one. And they have the boy, who I guess is the exact same age as me. I wonder what he thinks about all this?"

"Are you sure it's true?" Tara asked. "What else did they say? Do they want you to live with them or something?"

"I don't know. I don't think so. The man said he only just learned of it. His wife kept it a secret all this time. If he hadn't seen me at the coffee shop, I never would've known that the Simpsons weren't my real parents." Elizabeth told them the whole conversation she'd had with the Doyles.

"How did they…?"

"I don't know anymore than I'm telling you, Tara. I'm not sure I want to know more. I feel my life has been taken away from me twice. Once when my parents died, and now finding out they weren't even really my parents. It's almost just as much of a shock."

Megan put her arms around her and Elizabeth rested her head on her shoulder.

Tara stepped forward and rubbed her arm. "You've got us. We'll always stick together no matter what."

Elizabeth felt a little comforted by her friends.

"Are you curious to meet your other sister and the Simpson boy?" Tara asked.

"Yes, Elizabeth, he'd be just as upset as you. I'm guessing he didn't know before now, either. They likely just told him, too, and his birth parents are now dead."

"That's true. I can tell him everything I remember about them." She sighed. "All I want to do right now is tell Joseph what's happened.

"When do you see him next?" Tara asked.

Elizabeth leaned forward and stared at Tara's lips. "Have you been wearing lipstick?"

She rubbed at her lips with the back of her hand. "Just a little bit. Don't tell."

"I won't."

"I'm seeing Joseph tomorrow at eleven. If you could take me to the pond by the Eshs' farm, Tara?"

"Okay. I don't start work until two, but I guess I'd be able to find something to do in town." Tara's eyes sparkled with mischief. "You'll feel better with his big strong arms around you. Make sure to cry a little; that always works."

"Tara!" Megan was shocked.

Tara laughed. "Elizabeth should make the best of every situation."

"Why? Joseph already likes her."

"I'm just saying what I would do. Now help me with this buggy."

Elizabeth helped them unhitch the buggy and rub the horse down. Finding out who her parents were caused her to question who she was. It seemed odd that the past could affect the present so dramatically.

THE NEXT MORNING when Tara and Elizabeth arrived at the pond, Joseph was sitting in his buggy waiting.

"Don't forget what I told you!" Tara whispered before Elizabeth left the buggy.

"Thanks, Tara. I'll see you tonight."

When Tara drove the buggy on, Elizabeth ran to Joseph and told him everything she'd learned about her past and about the Simpsons not being her birth-parents.

He sat there staring at her. "That's awful, Elizabeth."

"In my mind, I'd already wondered if there was a connection between that woman who fainted and that man. She came there to the coffee shop to get a look at me."

"What are you going to do now?"

"I don't know. I think they're fake people with fake lives."

He rubbed his forehead. "They're your parents."

"She's a liar."

"Don't be so harsh."

"Easy for you to say."

"*Nee,* it's not. I know you're feeling awful that you were lied to, but maybe something drove your mother to it."

"Nothing's that drastic, not enough to give away your child. I'd never give mine away. I'd die for my children when I have them, and do anything to protect them."

He shrugged. "There's nothing you can do about it now. Did she say she was sorry?"

"She did."

"Did you forgive her?"

"Not yet. I forget what I said, but in my heart, I don't forgive her. And I don't know if I ever can. What made her do it?"

"What reason did she give? You told me she said she thought her husband wanted a boy."

"That can't have been the true reason."

"It probably was if she said so. She wouldn't have a reason to keep lying now that the truth has come out."

"Do you think so?"

Joseph nodded as he reached out and took hold of her hand. "This is the way I see it; you had parents who loved you that died. Then you came to the Grabers who love you as though you're their own. Now, you have another lot of parents who want to get to know you. So, in eighteen years, you have had three sets of parents who love you and want the best for you."

He pulled her hand to his lips and pressed his lips against the back of her hand while staring into her eyes. She didn't know whether it was the caress of his lips or his calming voice, but she started to feel a little more positive about her situation.

"That's true, but I don't know who I am now."

"You're the same person you were before you found out all this."

"You think so?"

He nodded. "Of course."

"Then why do I feel so murky inside and so betrayed?"

"I know it's not easy, but it's all in the way you look at things. You can look at it as though you've had three sets of parents who've loved you, or you can put all your attention on the lies and deceit part of it. Which do you prefer to think about?"

"The good part I guess, but how do I know I can trust these people again?"

"You could give them a chance. They might not be trustworthy and they might not be nice, but if you don't give them a chance you'll never know."

Elizabeth heaved a sigh. "They left their phone numbers with Gretchen."

"*Gut!* Call them when you're ready and go and meet the rest of the family."

"Come with me?"

"What?" Joseph laughed. "Why me?"

"See? You're just as nervous."

"Maybe so, but I'll go with you if you want me to."

"I do. I'll feel so much better if you're there with me." She put her head on his shoulder. "You're so clever and so wise."

He chuckled. "I'll remember that you said that here and now, so I can always remind you."

CHAPTER FIFTEEN

Let no corrupt communication proceed out of your mouth,
but that which is good to the use of edifying,
that it may minister grace unto the hearers.
Ephesians 4:29

"She has to know, Janice."

"Does she?"

"Elizabeth has called and we've arranged for her to come here on Christmas Eve. We can't keep it from my mother; we have to tell her now. I'm certain she already knows something's going on."

Janice sighed. "You know we don't get along. She'll use this as another reason to hate me."

"It doesn't matter; she has to be told."

"All right. I might as well get it over with."

That night before dinner was served, Janice went into the sitting room with her husband and found Charlotte reading a book.

She closed the book and placed it onto her lap and looked up at them. "Lyle, what are you doing home?" Charlotte looked between Lyle and Janice and watched them sit down on the couch opposite.

"We've got something to tell you," Lyle said.

"Go ahead. I'm listening."

Janice stared at Lyle, hoping he'd speak, and thankfully he broke the news.

"Lyle Junior is not really a Doyle."

Her beady eyes fixed on Janice. "I knew it! You faked that pregnancy. That boy never fitted in. He doesn't even look like a Doyle and as for his brain capacity…"

Lyle leaned forward and wagged a finger at his mother. "Mother! You best stop there. Lyle is our son in every way as far as I'm concerned, and he always will be."

Charlotte pouted and looked from her son to Janice. "Does he know he's adopted?"

"There's more to the story, Mother."

"Well, tell me. Out with it!"

Janice knew she'd have to take over. "You and Lyle, well, I thought Lyle wanted a boy—anyway, I swapped the girl I had with someone else's boy."

Charlotte's mouth fell open. "You gave your own child away?"

Janice nodded knowing that now Charlotte had a valid reason to detest her.

"Did you know about this, Lyle?"

"He only learned of it when he met Elizabeth, the daughter I gave away."

She frowned at Lyle. "Tell me what happened from the beginning and don't leave a single thing out."

They sat there and told Charlotte everything.

"We must bring this girl back into the family."

"It's not as easy as that. She's been eighteen years thinking her parents were other people and now she's been ten years living with the Amish family."

"Once she sees what we have to offer her, she'll stay with us. What's she like?"

Janice said, "She's a lovely girl and she looks very much like Georgia."

Charlotte could barely look at her when she was speaking. "Yes, Lyle already mentioned that when he said he saw her in that coffee shop." She looked across at Lyle. "We've got a lot to offer her, Lyle. You must see that Elizabeth comes back to us. Did you know that Elizabeth is a family name? It was your great grandmother's name."

"No. I didn't know that. Anyway, Elizabeth called us, and she's coming here to meet everyone on Christmas Eve. She's bringing a friend with her."

"An Amish friend?"

"Yes, a young man."

"We can't have that. If she marries an Amish man she'll stay there forever. You must do what you can do make certain that doesn't happen, Lyle. You must encourage her to end that relationship."

"I'll be back. I just have to make a few calls." Lyle left the room.

Janice stared after him not believing he could leave her alone with his mother.

"You of all people should know how one should make a good marriage, Janice. You've done well to marry my son. So many other women were after him and now you have everything you want."

"I've got my own money, Charlotte! I didn't marry Lyle for his money."

Charlotte turned up her nose. "All the same, you must make sure that Elizabeth does not marry someone Amish."

"Why not, if that's her choice?"

"Have you lost your senses, woman?"

"Charlotte, can you stop trying to control everyone? If Elizabeth chooses to stay with the Amish she can. If she chooses to marry someone, it's none of your business and it's certainly none of mine."

Charlotte's mouth dropped open. Janice was tempted to hurry out of the room to get away from the woman who'd continually caused her grief, but she stayed, standing her ground.

"I've never been spoken to like that by anyone in all my born days!"

"It's probably about time then."

"I'll have to tell Lyle how you spoke to me just now."

"I wouldn't."

"Why?"

"I told him how you harped on and on about him wanting a boy, so I'd be careful what you said if I were you. He might end up blaming you for this mess."

"Me? That's ridiculous."

"Is it? I remember you telling me that some women can only have girls."

"Yes, well that's true. Some women aren't capable of having boys."

"That's biologically unfounded, but you kept putting me down and hinting that Lyle would leave me if I didn't produce a son and an heir. When the reality was, he didn't care at all. You were the one who wanted a boy. So he could carry on the name."

"You're trying to turn this around, so it's my fault? You're unbelievable. I wish my son never got involved with you. I can't see what he sees in you."

"I know what you think of me and I no longer care. I'm admitting that I made a terrible mistake, and with Lyle's help, I'm trying to put it right for everyone's sake. You have to appreciate that it hasn't been easy for me to tell you this."

Lyle came back into the room and Charlotte changed her tune.

"Yes, dear. It must be awful for you."

Janice looked up at her husband to see a smile on his face at the idea that Charlotte and she were getting along.

"I'm okay. I feel better now that it's all out in the open," Janice said.

"How is Lyle taking it?" Charlotte asked. "And what do we know about his heritage?"

"Not much. We're hoping that Elizabeth can enlighten us about Lyle's family, the Simpsons."

Charlotte grimaced. "It's a waste giving him the same name. Lyle the Fourth. And he's not a Doyle at all. I always knew there was something odd about that boy."

"He is, Mother. Nothing's changed in our eyes. Lyle is still our son. He's still a Doyle and always will be a Doyle."

The old woman huffed. "But he's not really, so why should he have the same name as you, your father and his father before him?"

Janice butted in, "It's just a name. It's not really that important."

When Lyle put a hand on her knee, Janice realized she should've kept quiet.

147

"Not important! Not important to you maybe. You married into this family not appreciating our history —that's more than obvious to everyone."

Janice pressed her lips together and kept silent. Who was 'everyone?'

"I can't believe that a child with my blood running through her veins has been raised as a foster child." She scowled with her lips downturned.

Janice looked away, feeling bad for her daughter and hoping she hadn't had a bad life.

"I'll see how Magda's getting along with dinner."

Janice hurried out of the room, hoping her mother-in-law wouldn't say too many nasty things behind her back. Although, she expected she would.

CHAPTER SIXTEEN

And thou shalt love the Lord thy God with all thine heart,
and with all thy soul, and with all thy might.
Deuteronomy 6:5

Christmas Eve.

*M*amm opened Elizabeth's bedroom door. "Can I come in?"

"*Jah,* of course."

Gretchen sat down on her bed while Elizabeth braided her hair.

"Are you nervous about meeting your family?"

"I am. What if I disappoint them?"

"You could never disappoint anyone. They'll be thinking the same of you." Gretchen gave a chuckle.

"I'm looking forward to meeting Lyle Junior and telling him what I remember of his parents. That feels funny, to say that they were *his* parents."

"They were yours, too."

"I guess. I just wish I'd known the truth earlier." She popped her prayer *kapp* on her head. "The only place that I can call home is right here with you and *Dat*." She sat down on the bed next to Gretchen and put her arm around her.

A giggle bubbled out of Gretchen. "We've been blessed to have you."

"How many children have you had over the years?" Elizabeth asked.

"Quite a few. You were our first and then we had those two girls when you were around eleven."

"Jah, they only stayed a few months."

"Then after that, there was little Tom."

Elizabeth giggled, remembering the chubby three-year-old. "So, with Tara and Megan, that's around… that's six."

Gretchen nodded. *"Gott* has a plan for each of us. *Gott* wanted you with us."

Placing her arm around Gretchen's shoulder again, she said, "I'm glad to be here with you. There's no place I would rather have been raised. I've felt safe here."

"You've been a blessing to us."

"Is it ever hard looking after children who aren't yours?"

"We're all *Gott's kinner*. It doesn't matter how each of you came to be with us. We had our struggles with Tara when she first came, but now she's settled down."

"That's right. I remember how she kept running away."

"Until she realized she had nowhere to run to and she was better off here."

Hoofbeats sounded outside the house.

"That'll be Joseph," *Mamm* said.

"I'm so glad he agreed to come with me."

"How are you getting there?"

"Mr. Doyle said he'd send a car for us at six."

"Mr. Doyle? Is that what you're going to call him?"

"That's all I can call him. I know none of it was his fault, but I can't call the man Dad. I barely know him."

Gretchen nodded. "Don't put any pressure on yourself. You'll get to know them all in time. Give them a chance to get to know you, too. You can be a little too quiet sometimes. Speak your mind. Otherwise, they won't get to know the real you."

Elizabeth breathed out heavily. "Okay. Thanks for the advice. I'll do my best."

When they heard a knock on the front door, Elizabeth said, "I'll go down and let him in."

On the ride to the Doyles' house, Elizabeth clutched Joseph's hand. There was no way she could've done this alone. Gretchen's words ran through her head; she'd have to be bold and speak up to let these people get to know her. Too often she'd hold back and let others talk around her. Tara was the one who usually took the lead when they were in a crowd of people. What she needed was a good dollop of Tara's confidence.

The car drove through double iron gates and headed to a grand two-story home.

"Wow! Look at it," Joseph said.

"I think they have a lot of money," Elizabeth whispered.

Once they got to the front door, it opened and Mr. and Mrs. Doyle stood before them. Elizabeth introduced Joseph and then they were walked through the house to meet the others. The house opened into a huge foyer with a glass framed ceiling. From the center hung a huge crystal chandelier. Once Elizabeth pulled her eyes from that, they were drawn to a sweeping staircase leading to the next level. As they walked alongside the Doyles, Elizabeth couldn't help noticing the six-foot-high portraits of people in old-fashioned clothing. Were they her ancestors? It seemed odd to know almost nothing of the Simpsons, and here there was a wealth of family history to be learned. By learning more about the Doyles, she'd surely learn more about herself.

They were shown to a sitting room where the rest of the family waited for them. There was her grand-mother, Charlotte, her two sisters, Georgia and Felicity, and Lyle, the biological son of the people who'd raised her until she was eight.

Lyle was the first to speak after the introductions were done. "Tell me about my parents."

Elizabeth smiled as she remembered them. "Mom was always teaching me things. She taught me how to read and write before I went to school. Dad loved ice-skating. I think he was some kind of champion. There were trophies with little figures on top—gold and silver trophies."

"I knew he'd be athletic."

"You look a little like him, I think. I can't remember their faces now."

"Do you have any photos? Do you still have those trophies?"

"I had a box of things, but they were lost. I remember I had them at my second foster home, but I arrived at the Grabers' with nothing but my clothes. The Grabers asked about my things for me, but the case-worker said the other family didn't have anything of mine."

Lyle Junior nodded and smiled at her. He seemed nice, like the rest of them.

"I was told that both of my parents, Joseph and Lillian didn't have any relatives at all and I was going to check into that, but I haven't yet."

"I'll look into it," Lyle said. "Or, we could both do it."

"They did have a relative," Janice said.

All eyes gravitated to Janice.

"I remember that Margaret told me that Lillian was scared of hospitals and that's why she had her baby at her birthing center rather than a hospital. The recommendation to go to Margaret came from a doctor friend of Margaret's who was a distant relative to Lillian."

"A doctor relative. That's interesting," Lyle said. "I might go into medicine. I think I'd like that."

Charlotte frowned at him. "You're not capable of getting grades good enough."

"I could start over. I only got bad grades because I've not really seen where I'm headed, so nothing makes sense, but if I have a goal like being a doctor that'll be a different thing."

Charlotte sighed. "Well, we'll just have to wait and see how that turns out, won't we? It'll be more of your father's money you'll be burning through why you try to find something you're good at."

"I'll pay him back when I'm a famous surgeon. I might even go into research and find cures for diseases."

The oldest daughter, Felicity, nodded. "You can do anything, once you put your mind to it, Lyle."

"Thanks, sis."

"I'll ask Margaret who that doctor was and I'll look into things," Janice said.

"We shall see," Charlotte said. "Tell us about yourself, Elizabeth."

Everything left Elizabeth's head once all eyes were turned her way. She'd never been good at speaking in front of people. She recalled what Gretchen said to her; she must speak, so they get to know her. "I like to ice-skate. That's my favorite thing to do. I work in a coffee shop." She giggled. "That's right. You already know that. That's about all really. After the accident, I went to live with a foster family for a few weeks, and then another family for a short time before I was placed with the Grabers when I was a young girl of around seven or eight. I've been with them ever since."

"Are you going to stay with the Amish?" Georgia asked.

With Joseph sitting right beside her it was a difficult thing to answer. Part of her wanted to get to know about her roots, and the other part of her wanted to stay where she felt safe. "I'm not certain." She could sense Joseph's disappointment in her answer.

"Do you think you'll stay at the coffee shop forever?" Charlotte asked.

"I don't know. It's good to have a job to bring money in."

"You can live with us and you wouldn't have to work," Charlotte said. "What's another one for my son to support?"

"Forgive my mother, Elizabeth. We don't want to put pressure on you, but we want you to know that you've always got a home here. You're welcome here at anytime and I was going to tell you once you got a little comfortable with us that you're welcome here whether you want to visit or indeed live with us."

"Thank you. That's nice to know."

"Well, would you consider it? We have to find a way to make up for what Janice has done," Charlotte said.

Elizabeth noticed that Janice opened her mouth in shock while Lyle Senior and everyone else seemed equally disturbed at what Charlotte had said.

"Thank you for the offer. I'm getting used to the idea. It would be too soon to make any decisions."

The old woman leaned forward. "So, you will consider it, dear?"

"Yes." Elizabeth couldn't see herself moving there anytime soon, but felt pressured to say she'd think about it.

"Will you both come and have Christmas with us tomorrow?" Janice asked.

"Yes, that would be wonderful. We'd really like to get to know you," Felicity said while her other sister nodded, looking equally as excited.

"I don't know that we'd be able to," Elizabeth said giving Joseph a sideways glance. After he had looked at her blankly, she said, "Thank you, but I don't think we can."

"It's our birthdays, Elizabeth. It would be nice if you could make it. Could you spare us just a couple of hours? Maybe have lunch here? No pressure."

Elizabeth smiled at Lyle. He was relaxed and friendly and was a link to the parents she'd lost so long ago. "Okay. I think we could. What do you think, Joseph?"

Joseph nodded.

"Excellent!" the grandmother said.

"As long as that's okay with everyone." Elizabeth looked at Janice and Lyle Senior.

"We couldn't think of anything better," Lyle Senior said.

"We'd love it," Janice added.

CHAPTER SEVENTEEN

Commit thy works unto the Lord,
and thy thoughts shall be established.
Proverbs 16:3

*a*t the end of a tense night, Elizabeth and Joseph were driven back to the Grabers' house.

They walked inside and, since everyone was asleep and they were away from the ears of the driver, they were free to talk about the evening.

Elizabeth slumped into the couch and Joseph sat next to her.

"How are you feeling after all that?"

"I feel like everything is spinning out of control. Everything's moving so fast lately."

"I sensed a lot of tension in the house. Most of it coming from the granny."

Elizabeth laughed. *"Jah,* she's one used to getting her own way over things, and I don't think she likes Janice."

"No love lost between the pair, it seems. Did you really mean you'd think about living with them?"

"Nee, but what could I say?"

"Why did you agree to go back there tomorrow? Don't you want to spend Christmas day here with William and Gretchen?"

"I said we'd go for lunch. I'll be back here before the evening meal. You will go with me, won't you?"

He grimaced. "I'd rather not, but if you want me to go with you, I will."

Elizabeth heaved a relieved sigh. *"Denke.* I'm trying to like them, but all I do is stare at Janice and wonder how she could give me away. Then I look at Lyle Junior and wonder why she chose him over me."

"It was simply because she was desperate for a boy. She explained that."

"Words don't help take the hurt away. She can explain whatever she wants, but I can't help feeling hurt that another baby was chosen over me. How could she have done it?'

"I don't know."

"I have confusion over everything. What if I took one year to live with them and learn more about them? Then I'd learn more about myself." She wondered what it would be like to live in that home that was like a palace. There she could have everything she'd ever wanted.

Joseph pulled back. "You'd actually do that? Leave the community?"

"I never said I'd stay."

"I thought… I thought that you would. What would happen to us if you left?"

"I don't know. I haven't thought everything through."

"Perhaps it's best you go there by yourself tomorrow."

"*Nee*, I can't do this without you."

"I didn't say anything tonight. I barely uttered a word. You'd be more free to be yourself without me there."

She knew his feelings were hurt. He wanted to marry her; he'd made that known. If she married him, then her life would be set on a course with no turning back.

They would set up house, and together they'd raise a family. With Joseph, she knew how life would turn out. There was another road she could take. The road was unknown and her future uncertain if she went to live with the Doyles. Her insides felt hollow when she realized she couldn't marry Joseph without first exploring the other side of herself. The side of the person she might have become if she'd been raised as a Doyle.

"Tell me what you're thinking, Elizabeth. You've gone quiet again."

"There's a lot going on in my head. I've been thinking so much lately I feel like my head's going to burst. Lyle really wanted to know about his parents and I didn't have anything much to tell him. I don't even remember their faces, just vague impressions. I wish I still had that box of their belongings and photos. They were most likely thrown out."

"I'm not concerned about him; I'm concerned about you. As much as I want to protect you and be by your side, I think it's better if you go alone tomorrow. I'll come here in the morning to see you for Christmas and your birthday."

She nodded. "If you think that's best."

"I do. You've got some big decisions to make. I'll be around if you need to talk anything over with me."

She smiled at him. "You're the best."

"Don't forget it," he said with a cheeky wink. "Now, I better get home."

"Denke for coming with me today."

"You're welcome. Don't get up." He leaned over and kissed her softly on her forehead. "I'll see you tomorrow morning."

He walked out the door and then she was left alone, but not for long because as soon as she heard Joseph's buggy horse clip-clopping down the driveway, Tara rushed out of the kitchen toward her.

"What happened?" Tara asked as she sat down next to Elizabeth with her legs tucked under her.

"Were you hiding in the kitchen?"

"I had started to get myself some tea before you got home. I didn't mean to hide, but you didn't know I was there, so I didn't want to interrupt the two of you."

"What did you hear?"

"You're going back there tomorrow?"

"Just for lunch. You should've seen their grand home. They had ceilings that were so high I don't know how they got up there to clean them and I would hate to have to clean that huge staircase. I'm sure the floors

163

were made out of marble. I've never seen anything like it. Their house was like a museum."

"Elizabeth, you have all the luck. Why couldn't it have been me?" She leaned toward her. "I'd leave here in a heartbeat and make the most of being one of them. I'd love having them try to make up to me for all those lost years." Tara chuckled.

"Yeah, but if it really happened to you, you'd feel differently."

"I doubt it. Did they ask you to live there?"

"They said I was welcome to if I wanted."

"I know what I'd be doing. Want to swap?"

Elizabeth frowned at her.

"Oh, I'm sorry, bad choice of words."

"Yeah. Already been done. Why don't you come with me?"

"For real?"

"I'd feel so much better if I had you there. They think that Joseph is coming and so I'm sure they wouldn't mind."

"What about Megan?"

Elizabeth sighed. "Oh. She'd feel left out. I can't take the two of you."

"Best I don't go. Megan would feel left out."

"That's so nice of you, Tara. I wouldn't like Megan to feel bad. She's so sweet."

"I'm a nice person."

Elizabeth giggled. "I know you are."

"I hope you do."

"Would you ever leave?"

"I guess so. I don't know. I'm hesitant to leave the same as you are. We'll all have to make that decision now that we're all eighteen."

"That's true. It kind of crept up on me. I can't believe I'll be eighteen tomorrow."

"If I were you I'd see what their life is like. It's the life you should've had, Elizabeth."

"What concerns me is that I didn't have it. What if I didn't have it for a reason? William and Gretchen are always saying we're here for a reason. I believe that's true. This is where God wants me to be. But does He still want me here, or is it time for me to be somewhere else? What if He want's me with the Doyles?"

Tara shook her head. "I don't know."

"How do I find out?"

"That's a hard question. I don't know. Do you think you have to try and see? Maybe talk to Gretchen."

"I'll talk with her before I go there tomorrow. It'll be weird going there by myself."

"You'll be okay."

Elizabeth nodded. "I guess. They're sending a car for me at eleven."

Elizabeth had so many questions, but deep down, she didn't think anyone had the answers. She hoped that she'd get some direction tomorrow. As for now, the only thing she wanted was to crawl into her warm bed, pull the covers over her head and sleep.

CHAPTER EIGHTEEN

This book of the law shall not depart out of thy mouth;
but thou shalt meditate therein day and night,
that thou mayest observe to do according to all
that is written therein:
for then thou shalt make thy way prosperous,
and then thou shalt have good success.
Joshua 1:8

*O*n Christmas morning, Janice and Lyle had just woken when Lyle presented Janice with a gift.

Sitting in bed, she stared at the carefully wrapped gift in her hands. "I don't deserve anything after what I did."

"We all have to make an effort to put the past behind us."

She stared into her husband's eyes. "Does that mean you forgive me?"

"I do forgive you. That doesn't mean I'm not still shocked and trying to get my head around it. I know women have all kinds of hormones going on when they're pregnant, so maybe that was a good part of it."

"I don't know."

"Open it."

She pulled on one end of the red ribbon and the bow unraveled. Then she unwrapped it. It was a jewelry box. Janice opened it to see the diamond earrings she'd been admiring. "How did you know?"

"Travis told me."

Travis was their jeweler.

She picked up the delicate platinum and diamond drop earrings and held them up to the light. The sun shining in through the window broke into reflections of every color of the rainbow. "They're so pretty." She leaned over and kissed him. "Now you can open yours. I hope you like it. You're so hard to buy for."

"I told you, I don't need anything." He opened the present by his bedside. It was the latest designer watch by his favorite watchmaker. "Thank you." He clipped it onto his wrist. "I love it." He kissed her on her cheek.

She knew he was trying hard, but a wedge had developed between them. They'd grown distant, and finding out what she'd done had only caused more distance between them. Janice knew the only thing that would heal their relationship would be time and effort. He could've divorced her and never wanted to talk to her again, so she was grateful that he hadn't done that. That had to mean he was serious about their marriage.

"Are you going to put them on?"

She stared at him.

He frowned at her. "What were you thinking about? You go so quiet sometimes."

"Oh, I was just thinking about us. I just want things to go back to being the way they were when we first married."

"So many things have changed. We didn't have children when we were first married. We were on our own and more carefree. That's why I said we should travel. Then we wouldn't have so many day-to-day worries."

She smiled. "I'd like that."

"Are you going to put them on?" he asked again.

"I will." One after the other, she pushed them through the holes in her ears. "How do they look?"

"Stunning!"

She gave a little laugh.

"We've got a big day ahead. I hope Elizabeth doesn't change her mind. She seemed a little timid."

Janice gasped. "No. She won't change her mind, will she? That would be dreadful."

"I shouldn't have said anything. I hope not. It'll be good if she gets to know all of us."

"I hope she likes us. It must be like coming into a different world from the one she's been living in. I don't know how they all live in that dark little home."

"Whatever it is, that's the only home she's known for a long time. The one she's lived in most of her life. Did you call Margaret about finding out if the Simpsons have relatives? You mentioned that you thought they might have a doctor who's a relation?"

"I haven't talked to her, but I will."

"I thought you spoke to her nearly every day."

"I do, but there have been so many other things going on that I forgot to ask her. I'll find out today."

"Is she coming to the house?"

"No. She's visiting relatives in Connecticut for the holidays, but she's always got her mobile with her. I forgot to tell you something else; I've given Magda some time off from working today."

"Who's going to be cooking today?"

"We've got a chef coming in as well as other staff. Don't worry. It's been organized."

Elizabeth was shaken awake by Megan and Tara.

"What? What are you doing?" Elizabeth had never liked the early morning starts.

"Happy birthday," they chorused.

"Thank you. Now I need some more sleep." She rolled over hoping they'd leave her alone.

"You don't have a lot of time. Aren't they sending a car for you mid-morning?"

Elizabeth sat up. "What time is it?"

"Eight."

She flopped back into the pillow. "I suppose I should get up. Joseph is coming at eight thirty. The car isn't coming until eleven."

Right at eight thirty, Joseph arrived. She ran out to meet him.

"Have you changed your mind about coming with me today?"

He shook his head. "This is something you should do alone." He stepped closer and pulled her to him. "Happy birthday."

She pushed him away. "Stop. Someone will see."

"Come behind the buggy, then, so I can give you a birthday kiss."

She giggled. She'd never been kissed before and it would be perfect to be kissed on her eighteenth birthday by the man she wanted to marry.

"Do I have to beg?" he asked.

"Maybe?"

He pulled a sad face, so she stepped closer to him and pointed to her cheek. "You can kiss me there."

He stepped in and gently pressed his lips against her cheek.

When he finished, he stepped back. "I have a present I want to give you before we go inside."

"What is it?"

"You have to close your eyes."

She closed her eyes, and then peeked a little.

"Stop it! I saw that. No looking."

She closed her eyes again. "I'm not looking."

"Put out your arms."

Soon she felt something in her arms and she opened her eyes.

"Open it," he said.

She ripped the paper open to reveal a new set of skates. "They're beautiful." She looked them over. "And they're my size. How did you know?"

"It wasn't too hard. I just had a look at your old ones."

"I don't think I've ever had brand new skates like these. Thank you." She stepped closer and kissed him on his cheek.

"That's for your birthday, and not for Christmas. I'll take you shopping when the stores open again. I'm afraid I'm hopeless where gifts are concerned. I couldn't think what else you'd like."

"That's not necessary."

"It is. And it's a way I can spend more time with you."

She ran her hands across the white skates. "They're so lovely. I wish you could come with me today."

He placed both his hands on her shoulders. "Look at me."

Staring into her eyes, he said, "I've told you how I feel about you, but I don't want to influence your decisions about this family. You might want to live with them and leave the community."

"I know, you've explained it to me before, but I can still wish. Now come inside so I can give you your present."

"You got me a present?"

She giggled. "Of course I did. And I hope you like it." She led him back to the house thinking it funny that she'd also bought him skates.

When he got inside and opened them, he laughed. "Great minds think alike, they say."

"Well, I was hoping they would improve your skating because nothing could make it any worse."

. . .

ELEVEN O'CLOCK CAME and the car arrived. She said goodbye to everyone she loved and headed to the house of her newly discovered family.

On the way in the car she cried, and then she wiped her eyes the best she could so the driver wouldn't see. She was upset over Joseph. If he really loved her, he would've come with her and helped her through it. He'd said he didn't want to distract her, but didn't he love her enough to encourage her to stay within the community?

He'd never proposed to her, he just talked of marriage in a joking manner. If he had ever asked her properly to marry him, she would've said yes.

CHAPTER NINETEEN

Study to shew thyself approved unto God,
a workman that needeth not to be ashamed,
rightly dividing the word of truth.
2 Timothy 2:15

*I*t was hard for Elizabeth to walk up to the front door alone. Just as she reached it, it was flung open and once again Mr. and Mrs. Doyle stood there.

"Welcome," Mr. Doyle said as Mrs. Doyle leaned over and kissed her on her cheek.

"Isn't Joseph coming?" Mrs. Doyle said.

"He's, err. No."

"Well thank you for coming," Mr. Doyle said, ushering her inside. "We're all anxious to get to know you better."

She sat in the sitting room and talked with her sisters and Lyle Junior while the old grandmother eyed her from a distance and made her feel uneasy. As nice as her sisters and Lyle were, she still felt as though she didn't belong.

Lyle asked his questions about his birth parents, and she answered them as best she could.

Then a bell sounded and it was announced that the meal was ready.

Elizabeth walked with the others into a grand dining room. A long narrow table was filled with cut glass, silverware and fine china. After they sat, a waiter brought in a large turkey and then more food was brought out.

Mr. Doyle said a prayer of thanks while everyone closed their eyes.

Although Elizabeth was in glamorous and beautiful surroundings, her heart longed to be back in the small dark Amish farmhouse with mismatched plates and the plain wooden table surrounded by people she loved.

When she opened her eyes, Joseph was being shown into the room.

All eyes turned to him.

"I'm sorry I'm late," he said looking directly at Elizabeth and then looking at Mr. and Mrs. Doyle

Lyle and Janice stood up.

"That's no trouble at all. We'll seat you next to Elizabeth," Janice said.

Mr. Doyle pulled another chair from the corner of the room and placed it between Elizabeth and Felicity.

"I thought you weren't coming," Elizabeth whispered to him when he sat down.

"It didn't feel right without you. I got back home and all I wanted to do was spend the rest of the day with you."

One of the staff placed a table setting in front of him.

"I hope I haven't put anyone out by being late," Joseph said.

"Of course not. We're glad you were able to make it," Mr. Doyle said.

Joseph gave him an appreciative nod and then slid his hand under the table toward Elizabeth. She reached out and placed her hand in his.

She could get through anything with him beside her.

They ate a traditional Christmas dinner, with turkey and roasted vegetables and ham—all the foods she would've eaten at Gretchen's house, although there was a lot more of everything. Their dessert was traditional Christmas plum pudding, with ice cream, cream and brandy sauce. Afterward, liquor chocolates and coffee were served.

The Doyles knew already that Elizabeth was expected elsewhere so when the meal was over, they knew she had to go and they said their goodbyes.

When Elizabeth and Joseph got back to the Grabers' house, snow was lightly falling. Elizabeth watched the car that drove them there get smaller and smaller on the road. It was just at dusk.

"Don't go inside yet, Elizabeth."

"We have to; it's freezing."

"No more than usual." He grabbed her hand and ran with her to the barn where his horse and buggy were waiting. "I didn't come with you because I wanted you to make up your mind and feel no ties to the community, not to have you stay in the community out of guilt or out of your fondness for the Grabers." He looked upward. "I didn't think this would be so hard."

"What?"

"I want to marry you, Elizabeth. What do you think about that?" He shook his head. "Oh boy. That wasn't good."

She giggled. "Start again. Like how you started over when we first met."

"Elizabeth, will you marry me? I just need to let you know how I feel so you have all the facts and everything will be out in the open. I always want to…"

"Shh."

He stopped talking.

"Kiss me?"

"Is that a yes?" he asked.

"I wouldn't let you kiss me if it weren't."

He smiled, and stepped toward her and gently lowered his lips until they met hers. She closed her eyes, enjoying his soft lips against her own. When he lifted his head she looked into his blue eyes.

"When I saw you walk into the house tonight, I was so happy I felt I would burst. That was the best gift I've ever had. It meant the world."

He smiled. "I'm glad. I honestly never thought I'd meet a girl like you. I don't want to keep you from your family; that would be selfish."

"You're not. Janice gave birth to me, but other people raised me. You're my family now and so is the community. William and Gretchen always said that *Gott* wanted all the children who came through their *haus* to be there. I know that now, and I'm no longer angry with Janice. How could I be? If it weren't for what she did, I would never have met any of the people who are so dear to me now. And I wouldn't have met you."

Joseph took hold of her hand and brought it up to his lips and kissed it. "I knew I'd marry you the very first time I saw you."

For the first time since she learned the dreadful news, she felt whole. It was true what she'd said to Joseph, she no longer felt anger or resentment because it had all been God's will.

CHAPTER TWENTY

Commit thy way unto the Lord;
trust also in him; and he shall bring it to pass.
Psalm 37:5

That night across town.

"*How* ow do you think tonight went? Do you think Elizabeth will ever want to come and live with us?"

Lyle Senior and Janice were sitting alone in one of their sitting rooms after everyone had gone to bed.

Lyle pressed his lips together and shook his head. "I strongly doubt it. She seems very fond of that young man."

"He seems nice. He's very polite."

"It was nice for Lyle to learn a little about his birth parents."

"I feel better about things now that they're out in the open. I thought you'd divorce me for certain."

"Janice, you have to forgive yourself."

She nodded.

"We have to look into the legalities of Lyle and Elizabeth's birth certificates and get them changed. I didn't want to raise that subject tonight. It wasn't the right time."

"Yes. That'll have to be made right. I didn't even think of that."

"It certainly makes me see that the two of us have suffered from a lack of communication. I've been too focused on work and you must say what's on your mind instead of worrying all the time. That's what causes some of your headaches."

"I'll try."

"Never mind trying, just do it."

Janice sighed. "Okay."

"It's been a big day, but I believe a successful one."

"Yes, another Christmas day is over and it was one like no other. I hope Elizabeth always keeps in touch with us. In a way, I feel that we owe it to the Simpsons to watch over both of them, Lyle Junior and Elizabeth."

"Of course, they're both ours. We'll have to take things at her pace, though."

"Did you see she hugged me when she was leaving tonight?"

He smiled. "I did. She relaxed by the end of the night. Janice, I guess I don't say it often enough, but I love you."

Tears stung at the back of her eyes. He'd not told her that for years. "I love you too."

"Let's make these last years count."

She laughed. "We've not gotten that old yet."

"I know, but this whole business has made me realize that I've been taking everything for granted—you and the children. I want to make things right."

"All I ever wanted was to make you happy and be a good wife."

He pulled her close and put his arm around her. "You have made me happy and I'm going to spend the next years making you know it." Lyle kissed her on her forehead and she rested her head against him.

Shall we tell them we're going to get married?" Joseph looked at the Grabers' house.

"*Nee,* we'll keep it to ourselves for a little while."

"I want the world to know."

Elizabeth giggled, and then whispered, "Keep quiet! You're too noisy."

"You're not going to change your mind, are you?"

"Is that why you want to tell everyone?"

"Uh huh. That way, you'll be locked in."

She giggled again. "I'm locked in now."

"We better go inside, then or I'll have to kiss you again."

She ducked away from him and ran to the house. "Last one's last."

He ran after her and got to the door at the same time as she.

"Let's tell them tonight if you want to," she said.

"We'll get married at the end of January and my *bruder* will help me build us a *haus.*"

"You've got it all figured out."

"That's all I've thought about these past weeks. I started planning everything when I met you. I couldn't risk losing you to the Doyles."

"I'll see them again, but you'll never lose me to anyone."

Elizabeth's thoughts went to the Simpsons who'd raised her and given her love. They had to be with God; she was certain of it. Now looking through the window at the Christmas tree and the soft light from the candles in the windows, she knew her life was full, and her future was with Joseph. Everything had come together on her birthday, Christmas Day. Eighteen years ago, a decision changed her life and put it on a different course.

Just as Joseph put his hand on the door handle, she said a silent prayer of thanks to God for her life turning out exactly how it had.

Thank you for reading Amish Girl's Christmas.

www.SamanthaPriceAuthor.com

THE NEXT BOOK IN THE SERIES.

If you'd like to find out what happens next with the Grabers and the foster girls, the next episode is
Book 2:
Amish Foster Girl

Two young men have set Tara's heart racing; one is quiet and plain, and the other is handsome and confident. A respected member of the Amish community hints that one of the men is untrustworthy, but which man?
Can
Tara choose a husband without getting caught up in appearances?
(4 book series).

ABOUT SAMANTHA PRICE

Samantha Price is a USA Today bestselling and Kindle All Stars author of Amish romance books and cozy mysteries. She was raised Brethren and has a deep affinity for the Amish way of life, which she has explored extensively with over a decade of research.

She is mother to two pampered rescue cats, and a very spoiled staffy with separation issues.

www.SamanthaPriceAuthor.com

ALL BOOK SERIES

Amish Maids Trilogy
A 3 book Amish romance series of novels featuring 5 friends finding love.

Amish Love Blooms
A 6 book Amish romance series of novels about four sisters and their cousins.

Amish Misfits
A series of 7 stand-alone books about people who have never fitted in.

The Amish Bonnet Sisters
To date there are 28 books in this continuing family saga. My most popular and best-selling series.

Amish Women of Pleasant Valley

An 8 book Amish romance series with the same characters. This has been one of my most popular series.

Ettie Smith Amish Mysteries
An ongoing cozy mystery series with octogenarian sleuths. Popular with lovers of mysteries such as Miss Marple or Murder She Wrote.

Amish Secret Widows' Society
A ten novella mystery/romance series - a prequel to the Ettie Smith Amish Mysteries.

Expectant Amish Widows
A stand-alone Amish romance series of 19 books.

Seven Amish Bachelors
A 7 book Amish Romance series following the Fuller brothers' journey to finding love.

Amish Foster Girls
A 4 book Amish romance series with the same characters who have been fostered to an Amish family.

Amish Brides
An Amish historical romance. 5 book series with the same characters who have arrived in America to start their new life.

Amish Romance Secrets

The first series I ever wrote. 6 novellas following the same characters.

Amish Christmas Books
Each year I write an Amish Christmas stand-alone romance novel.

Amish Twin Hearts
A 4 book Amish Romance featuring twins and their friends.

Amish Wedding Season
The second series I wrote. It has the same characters throughout the 5 books.

Gretel Koch Jewel Thief
A clean 5 book suspense/mystery series about a jewel thief who has agreed to consult with the FBI.

Made in United States
Troutdale, OR
11/21/2023

14798512R00111